To Be YOUNG IN AMERICA

GROWING UP WITH THE COUNTRY ★ 1776–1940

Little, Brown and Company

Time Warner Book Group
1271 Avenue of the Americas, New York, NY 10020
Visit our Web site at www.lb-kids.com

First Edition: July 2005

Library of Congress Cataloging-in-Publication Data

Cole, Sheila.
To be young in America : growing up with the country 1776–1940 / by Sheila Cole.— 1st ed.
    p. cm.
ISBN 0-316-15196-3
    1. United States—Social life and customs—Juvenile literature.
    2. United States—Social conditions—Juvenile literature.
    3. Children—United States—Social life and customs—Juvenile literature.
    4. Children--United States—Social conditions—Juvenile literature.
    5. Children—United States—Biography—Juvenile literature.
    I. Title.

E161.C65 2005
973—dc22   2004015109

10 9 8 7 6 5 4 3 2 1

TWP

PRINTED IN SINGAPORE

Cover & interior layout by YAY! Design
The text was set in Filosophia.

To Be Young in America

in America

GROWING UP WITH THE COUNTRY

1776–1940

SHEILA COLE

LITTLE, BROWN AND COMPANY

New York · Boston

FOR MY DEAR FRIENDS
EDIE GELLES & JILL NORGREN

Contents

Acknowledgments

This book would not have come into being without the help of many people who inspired and encouraged me, gave me advice and information, and helped me find the materials I needed to complete it. To all of them I owe a deep debt of gratitude.

Edie Gelles and Jill Norgren were, in large part, responsible for inspiring me to write this book. Both of them are social historians and biographers and both have been my friends for years. Our conversations led me to read widely in American social history. It was not a long journey from their interest in the history of women and families to the history of American children. Once I had made that journey, the idea of writing a book about growing up in America for young people seemed like a natural next step. I was encouraged during the long process of turning an idea into a book by the example and support of my "writing buddies," Kathy Krull and Jean Ferris. My husband and friend, Michael Cole, has helped me in more ways that I can count. His generosity and love make everything possible.

My agent Jennifer Flannery believed in the book before it was born, and she convinced Megan Tingley to believe in it, too. I am grateful to both of them for their faith in me and this project. Megan helped to give shape to my idea. She knew before I did what I needed to do to realize my vision, but being the superb editor she is, she left me the room and time to discover things for myself. Mary Gruetzke lent a hand to shaping the book in its early stages. Andrea Spooner has shepherded it through further drafts with patience, good humor, and an eye for detail. I thank them all.

No book like this would be possible without libraries, librarians, and archivists. The libraries of the University of California and the California State University systems are a treasure trove for any researcher. The University of California, San Diego librarians have always been there to help when I needed them and were gracious about doing so. I am grateful to the American Antiquarian Society, the New York Historical Society, and the Southern Historical Collection of the University of North Carolina, Chapel Hill for their inter-library loan services as well as their courteous, competent staffs. I would also like to thank the staffs of the many museums and historical societies where I obtained illustrations and photographs for their help. Thanks also to the webmasters and others responsible for the listserve at H-CHILDHOOD@H-NET.MSU.EDU.

Introduction ∼ Looking into the Past

When I was growing up, an old photograph that hung on the wall of my parents' bedroom fascinated me. In it, my grandmother, whom I knew only as an old lady, is a young woman. Standing beside her is my grandfather, who died shortly after I was born. My mother, who died in 2001, is just a baby sitting on my grandfather's knee.

Taken in 1913, in Poland, the photograph captures a moment in time that I like to think of as "the beginning of the story" — my mother's story and mine. In the picture, it is before World War I, before the historical events that would make my mother leave her home and her family when she was fourteen years old to come, by herself, to America. The stage was set, but the story of my mother's life was still to unfold.

When looking through old picture albums, I always pause at the pictures of young people and wonder who they were and what their stories were. Did they go to school? To work? What kinds of games did they play? What happened to them when they grew up? While most American history books tell you about presidential elections, the fight over slavery, the settlement of the West, or the building of the railroads, they are silent when it comes to young people's lives. They do not tell you what it was like to be fifteen years old in 1776 and to join the militia to fight the British. Nor do they tell you what happened to children when they broke the law, became sick, went to school, or went to work, or what happened when their parents died. Yet children have been there throughout our history — working, playing, learning, trying to make sense of events, taking care of themselves, making trouble, finding friends, flirting, and becoming the next generation of adults.

This book tells you what it was like to be young and how the process of growing up has changed over the course of our nation's history. It concentrates on the period from 1776 to 1940 because it was during those years — when the United States was becoming a powerful, industrialized nation — that young people's lives were changing dramatically. Many of your own experiences growing up today are the continuation of those trends.

In a country as diverse as the United States, what children's lives are like depends on who they are, when and where they live, their gender, and their ethnic, racial, and religious backgrounds, as well as their parents' economic situation. Growing up in the 1820s in Boston was not the same as growing up on a farm in Ohio or Alabama. African-American children, both slave and free, have had fewer educational and work opportunities and harder lives than most European-American children.

This book describes how the lives of young people have been influenced by such events as wars, industrialization, urbanization, the spread of technology, and the beginning of compulsory education. As important as these large-scale events are for understanding children's lives, they are not enough to understand how actual children experienced them. To do this, I have included the stories of eight young people who lived in different times in our nation's history. Each of them was remarkable in some way, yet their experiences of growing up were like those of many other young people of their day. I believe that these personal stories and the information about the trends and forces that affected children's lives offer a more human perspective on our history.

At Home

GROWING UP ON THE FRONTIER

Daniel Drake (1785–1852)

On an early spring day in 1794, Daniel Drake was sitting bareback on a lazy horse watching two squirrels chasing each other. Without warning, the horse came to an abrupt halt as the plow it was pulling caught on a root, pitching Daniel onto the horse's collar and knocking the wind out of him. The pain brought tears to his eyes. The blow to his stomach was all that was needed to make a bad day worse.

Only half an hour before, Daniel had been sitting with the other children in the little log cabin school near the town of Mayslick, Kentucky. He had just been chosen to go fetch water from the spring — an honor all the boys vied for — when his father burst into the schoolroom. Mr. Drake had come to take Daniel from the school to help him with the plowing, for he found it impossible to manage both the horse and plow on the piece of land that had just been cleared.

This was the second time Daniel's father had taken him out of school. The first was when he needed help clearing the land. Daniel's father was too poor to hire a laborer. So Daniel was given a small ax, while his father had a larger one and a mattock (a tool for cutting up roots). With these tools and some bread and meat wrapped in a towel, Daniel and his father went off to clear the forest. Daniel's father did the heavy chopping. It was Daniel's job to hack down the saplings, cut off the tree branches, and pile the brush into heaps to be burned.

They built a sixteen-by-twenty-foot cabin on the land they cleared with a single room in which the whole family lived. The Drake family was poor and had few possessions. Daniel's winter clothing consisted of a suit of butternut-colored linsey-woolsey (linen and wool), a woolen hat, a pair of mittens, and a pair of old stocking legs drawn down like gaiters over his shoes to keep out the snow.

It was a lonely existence, but it drew the family closer together and made them appreciate the visitors who came their way.

After the land was cleared, Daniel helped his father with the planting, weeding, and harvesting. From the age of eight until he was fifteen, he tended the family's horses, cows, pigs, and sheep. In winter, when his father was short of fodder, he had to take the animals to the woods to browse during the day and hunt them up and drive them home again at night.

In the morning after he fed the livestock, Daniel was called on to watch the johnnycake baking on an ash board in front of the fire and to set the table. While his mother sat nursing the baby in the corner, his sister Lizzie dressed the little ones. When the johnnycake was done, Daniel would blow the conch shell for his father to come in from the field for breakfast. Then the family would gather around the table and recite the blessing. While they were eating, his father and mother would be talking of crops and livestock, and whether "Dannel," as they called him, could be spared from the house.

Daniel was the oldest child in the family, and while the others were still young, it was his job to provide the sauce — or the vegetables — for dinner. He also had to help with the girls' chores — milking the cows, churning butter, making cheese, and doing laundry — until his sisters were old enough to take those chores over from him.

After the Drake family moved from Mayslick to the cabin in a clearing in the woods, days would pass when they saw no one except each other. It was a lonely existence, but it drew the family closer together. It also made them appreciate the visitors who did come their way. "The visit of a boy, even on business, was a matter of delight," Daniel recalled.

The Drake family was religious and they often felt God's presence in their little clearing in the woods. Sometimes during a summer thunderstorm, when raindrops or hailstones pelted the cabin roof, his parents would open the Bible and read. "We might be destroyed; but another and purer emotion blended with our fears — a feeling of reverence converting terror into awe. We were in the midst of a great and sudden visitation of Divine power," Daniel Drake wrote, recalling those times.

Daniel Drake's parents spoke with one voice when it came to raising their children. They were gentle but firm. Daniel's father talked to the children about life and good and evil when they were working with him out in the fields. When Daniel was seven years old, a neighbor complained to Daniel's father that the boy had pulled up his cucumbers. Daniel's father told him that stealing was "very wicked" and that he could be sent to jail — a big, dark place where he would be all alone.

Daniel's mother did not hesitate to tell her children when she thought they had sinned. Her rules were simple: "The Bible forbids this, and commands that, and God will punish you if you act contrary to his word!" In the midst of their never-ending household duties, Daniel recalled that she would remind her

Daniel Drake

(Ohio Historical Society)

children that it was wicked "to treat anything which had life with cruelty — it was wicked to neglect the cattle or forget the little lambs in winter — it was wicked to waste or throw away bread or meat — it was wicked to strike or quarrel with each other. . . . It was wicked to be lazy — to be disobedient — to work on the Sabbath — to tell a falsehood, to curse and swear, to get drunk or fight."

Daniel's father had great respect for learning. He wanted at least one of his children to have a better life than that of a common farmer, although he could not afford to educate all of them. He decided to make Daniel, who was the eldest, into a doctor. But before that could happen, Daniel had to go back to the local school to complete his studies. Since he was still needed on the farm, Daniel rose at dawn every day and worked in the field till breakfast time. Then, after rushing through breakfast, he ran the two miles to school.

When he was fifteen years old, Daniel left the farm to go to Cincinnati to study medicine. It was a great sacrifice for the family to give up Daniel's help when he was strong enough to do a man's work on the farm.

Daniel Drake made good on his father's dreams for him, becoming a well-known doctor and a professor of medicine at Transylvania University in Lexington, Kentucky.

Adapted from Daniel Drake, Pioneer Life in Kentucky: 1785–1800.

At Home

I asked a boy I know what his mother did. The boy, who was trying to be clever, told me that his mother walked the dog and picked up its poop. When I looked surprised, he admitted that she also went to the grocery store, cooked, and took care of things. His sister interrupted. "She's a lawyer," she said, as if that ended the discussion. But she couldn't tell me what her mother did as a lawyer because she was in school all day while her mother was at her office practicing law.

The lives of most children today overlap with their parents' lives, but they are mostly separate from them. Boys and girls go to school, while their parents go to work in offices miles from home. There are many things they do not know about each other. The kids have friends who are their own age, while their parents have their own friends. Children usually have only a hazy idea of what their family's finances are like, and they know just a few of their parents' worries and dreams. Even though they love their mother and father, they are not able to do much to help them cope with their concerns or achieve their dreams, aside from being understanding and cooperative.

FIGURE 1.1 *There was little furniture in most early nineteenth century houses, and even in wealthier homes, few children slept alone. Poorer families all ate out of a common pot.* (August Kollner, *Pennsylvania Country Life*, 1840. Chicago Historical Society)

FAMILIES TODAY AND YESTERDAY

This state of affairs is a far cry from the way it was when Daniel Drake was growing up on the Kentucky frontier more than two hundred years ago. Back then, children were involved in almost all aspects of adult life — good and bad. The majority of Americans lived on farms and in small villages where, like the Drake family, parents and children worked together to produce everything they needed — including their food, clothes, tools, houses, and household furnishings. They traded or bartered for the things they could not grow or make themselves, like shoes

FIGURE 1.2 *Young men like the one pictured here took up space in the home and food off the table. To make room for the younger children, he would leave to live with others and work for his keep, or to attend school as Daniel Drake did.*

(Thomas Hovenden, *Breaking Home Ties*, 1890. Gift of Ellen Harrison McMichael in memory of C. Emory McMichael. Philadelphia Museum of Art)

WHO IS IN Your FAMILY?

Blended families with stepparents, stepsisters and stepbrothers, and half-sisters and half-brothers may sound modern, but in the nineteenth century, many children were members of such families. Instead of resulting from a parent's remarriage after divorce, these families came into being when one parent died and the remaining parent remarried.

Few couples divorced in the 1800s or early 1900s. Unhappily married men and women separated informally or abandoned their families. Often the father of the family left his wife and children when the family was going through a difficult period financially. In the days without the Internet, telephone directories, or Social Security numbers, it was not hard for a man or woman to disappear and never be heard from again.

and rum. They lived crowded together, often in one or two small rooms with little privacy, so that it was hard for children to avoid overhearing their parents' conversations or knowing what worried them.

Except for babies and those who were sick, almost everyone worked. Children began helping their parents with the household chores when they were four or five years old. By the time they were thirteen years old, many boys and girls were making substantial contributions to their families' welfare. And if needed, they helped their parents either by working for them or by paying someone else to work in their place even after they had left home. Boys and girls might go away to study, learn a trade, or work for someone else while they were in their teens, but they were still expected to obey their parents until they set up their own households, which was usually when they were in their twenties.

Not only did children work alongside their parents, but they also prayed and worshipped with them. They did not go to special Sunday school classes as children do today; they went to church with their parents, where they sat through long sermons. They played with their friends and with their brothers and sisters, but they also went with their parents to visit kin and neighbors. Along with their families, they attended community festivities at harvest parties, barn raisings, and weddings.

Life went on this way for many farm families until the twentieth century. But for some families, this way of life started to change in the years following the American Revolution as the country began to industrialize. As manufacturing and trade grew, goods like cloth and shoes became more readily avail-

Hiring the Family

Families often worked together in cotton mills, factories, and mines, just as they had worked together on the farm. Samuel Slater's factory in Oxford, Massachusetts, placed the following ad in *The Massachusetts Spy* on May 27, 1818:

FAMILY WANTED

Wanted at Samuel Slayter's [sic] Factory, in Oxford, a FAMILY with 5 or 6 Children, to work the Mills. One that has worked in a Mill would be preferred. Good recommendations will be required. Apply at the Factory Oxford

— May 20, 1818

able. To buy these things, farmers began to raise crops that they could sell at market to city dwellers for cash. Some families gave up farming altogether and moved to towns, where they took jobs in trade and in the industries that were springing up.

GROWING UP POOR

In some families, parents and children worked alongside one another in family businesses or in places like cotton mills just as they had when they lived on the farm. But more and more,

FIGURE 1.3 *A corn husking. All hands — from the smallest child to the eldest grandparent — pitched in to help with the work and took part in the fun.*

(Alvan Fisher, *Corn Husking Frolic*, 1828. Gift of Maxim Karolik for the M. and M. Karolik Collection of paintings, 1815–1865; photograph © Museum of Fine Arts, Boston)

FIGURE 1.4 *This family lived in two rooms in a New York tenement house in 1910. Notice that the room that they are sitting in is also the children's bedroom and the kitchen. The other room with the double bed was where the parents and the baby slept and where clothes were stored.*

(Jesse Tarbox Beals, "Room in a Tenement Flat," 1910. Jacob A. Riis Collection, Museum of the City of New York)

working-class men's jobs took them away from their families. They no longer worked alongside their children and taught them jobs as their parents had taught them. Nevertheless, many working-class families still had to depend on their children's help to keep a roof over their heads and food on the table. Most poor families had little in the way of savings. An accident, illness, or long layoff from work could push a family into poverty. Often, the only thing standing between a family and hunger and homelessness were the wages of their older children.

Discipline in working families tended to be harsh. Mothers and fathers who were hard-pressed to pay the landlord and put food on the table seldom had patience to reason with their children when they were unruly. When their children did not do as they were told, tired, overburdened parents were likely to yell or even lash out at them with their hands.

Anne Ellis, who grew up in a Colorado mining town in the 1880s, recalled that there was never any affection shown by her

FIGURE 1.5 *The furnishings of this prosperous city family's parlor included carpets, paintings and a big library. Compared to the spare interiors of the country cabin pictured in Figure 1.1, it is the height of luxury. In the days before radio and television, many families entertained themselves by reading aloud.*

(*Christian Family Magazine*, New York, Frontispiece, 1843. Old Sturbridge Village)

mother, "except that I have seen her love the latest baby, or gather the one next to it in her arms, deploring the fact that he had to be weaned, 'and only a little un yoreself.'" Hugging, kissing, and other displays of affection between children and their parents were rare in many families besides Anne Ellis's. But this did not mean that parents and children did not love each other or enjoy good times together. Many evenings, Anne and the other children gathered around the stove while their mother sewed and their stepfather read them stories or played the violin and sang for them.

Most working-class families were immigrants who began pouring into the country in the early nineteenth century. Every immigrant group faced the challenges of life in America in its own way, but there were some common threads. In the struggle to gain a foothold in America, it was not unusual to put the family's needs before those of any of its members. The elders in such a family might decide that the oldest daughter had to leave school and work in a factory so that her brothers could stay in school, or that the youngest daughter should not marry because she had to take care of Papa and the boys after Mama died.

Sons were more likely to be sent out to work than were daughters because boys were paid more money than their sisters. But that was not the only reason. Parents wanted their daughters at home, where they could keep an eye on them.

FIGURE 1.6 *By the 1880s, middle-class and wealthy families, like the one pictured here, typically had about four children. Notice that the father is not in the picture. Many wealthy and middle-class fathers were distant figures in their children's lives.*

(Michele Gordigiani, "Cornelia Ward Hall and Her Children," bequest of Martha Hall Barrett, Museum of the City of New York)

At home, girls helped their mothers care for the younger children, and they did housework, laundry, and piecework. (Piecework is the practice of paying a worker by the finished piece, whether it was making paper flowers, umbrellas, matches, or straw hats, or sewing linings or buttons on coats.)

IN COMFORTABLE CIRCUMSTANCES

With the growth of industry and trade, a new kind of family life began to develop among more prosperous families living in cities and towns. In this kind of family, which is like many families today, parents and children did not work together as a unit to support the family. Fathers left their wives and children at home and went to work in offices, mercantile establishments, factories, and workshops, where they earned the money to buy goods and services for their families.

Fathers were still the heads of these families. But since they were away all day, they could not help raise their children as they had when they were with their children for a large part of the day. Mothers kept the house, raised the children, and disciplined them. Fathers were called in only as a last resort. "Wait until your father hears about this," mothers might say when they wanted to impress upon their children the seriousness of their misbehavior.

Children in this new kind of family were expected to bring joy to their parents by being obedient boys and girls who were loving and kind. Since they did not work, they had

FIGURE 1.7 *This 1890 picture of a mother paddling her child is an advertisement for a Red Cross base burner. Children were spanked for doing things such as hurting their brothers or sisters, stealing, using bad language, or doing something considered to be dangerous.*

(Courtesy The Winterhur Library: Joseph Down Collection of Manuscripts and Printed Ephemera)

more free time than children had ever had before. In place of working alongside their mothers and fathers, they were given little chores around the house to train them to be helpful. They visited and played with other children instead of going visiting with their parents. They had parties to which other children were invited. On Sundays, they went to religious school for children rather than sitting through long sermons with adults.

CHILDREN: SINFUL OR INNOCENT?

Just as family life was changing, so were beliefs about the nature of children. By the time of the American Revolution, the belief that children were born sinful was out of fashion with many of the colonists. The English philosopher John Locke argued that children's characters and habits were shaped by their experiences, by the people they knew, and by their training. This idea appealed to Americans, who were creating a new country based on the ideals of equality and individual liberty.

A LITTLE PERSUASION

This new way of thinking about children made mothers more responsible than ever before for their children's behavior. Many mothers turned to their clergymen, the Bible, and child-rearing books for advice on how to raise their children to be obedient, hardworking, God-fearing people.

How Many CHILDREN?

At the time of the American Revolution, a typical woman had an average of seven or eight children. During the nineteenth century, many women began to have fewer children and to space the births of their children closer together than they had in the past. By 1900, the average woman was having only four children. During the Great Depression of the 1930s, when millions of people were out of work, the typical family had only two children. The average American family in the year 2000 had two children, but many families had only one child.

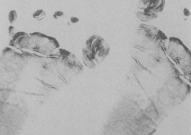

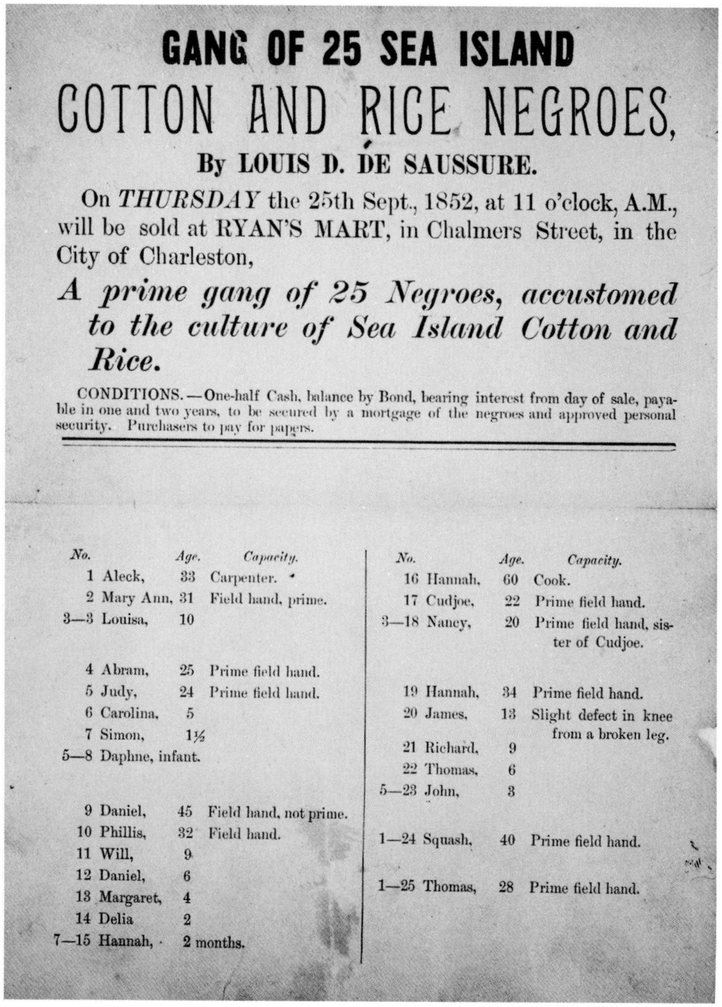

GANG OF 25 SEA ISLAND
COTTON AND RICE NEGROES,
By LOUIS D. DE SAUSSURE.

On *THURSDAY* the 25th Sept., 1852, at 11 o'clock, A.M., will be sold at RYAN'S MART, in Chalmers Street, in the City of Charleston,

A prime gang of 25 Negroes, accustomed to the culture of Sea Island Cotton and Rice.

CONDITIONS.—One-half Cash, balance by Bond, bearing interest from day of sale, payable in one and two years, to be secured by a mortgage of the negroes and approved personal security. Purchasers to pay for papers.

No.		Age.	Capacity.
1	Aleck,	33	Carpenter.
2	Mary Ann,	31	Field hand, prime.
3—3	Louisa,	10	
4	Abram,	25	Prime field hand.
5	Judy,	24	Prime field hand.
6	Carolina,	5	
7	Simon,	1½	
5—8	Daphne, infant.		
9	Daniel,	45	Field hand, not prime.
10	Phillis,	32	Field hand.
11	Will,	9	
12	Daniel,	6	
13	Margaret,	4	
14	Delia,	2	
7—15	Hannah,	2 months.	

No.		Age.	Capacity.
16	Hannah,	60	Cook.
17	Cudjoe,	22	Prime field hand.
3—18	Nancy,	20	Prime field hand, sister of Cudjoe.
19	Hannah,	34	Prime field hand.
20	James,	13	Slight defect in knee from a broken leg.
21	Richard,	9	
22	Thomas,	6	
5—23	John,	3	
1—24	Squash,	40	Prime field hand.
1—25	Thomas,	28	Prime field hand.

FIGURE 1.8 *In this advertisement for the sale of slaves, the slaves are listed in what appears to be family groups. We do not know if the seller was willing to break up the families.*

("Slavery," 1852. Gift of John Washburn, Chicago Historical Society)

First, mothers were advised to show their unhappiness with disobedient children by speaking to them kindly. If they continued to disobey, they were told not to talk to the children. And if the silent treatment didn't do the trick, they were to try to make the children feel guilty and to refuse to give them anything to drink or eat. Spanking, hitting, and beating were a last resort.

There is no way to know how many parents actually followed this advice. Mary Walker, who lived on the Oregon frontier in the 1840s, wrote an account in her diary of how she tried to teach her two-year-old son Cyrus to obey her after he refused to say "please" when he asked for some sugar. First, she spanked him, then his father spanked him. Exhausted from crying, Cyrus fell asleep. When he woke up, he was asked again if he would say please. "I don't want to say please," the two-year-old told his parents; they put him to bed hungry. The next morning, when Cyrus still refused to say please, he was spanked again until his parents were afraid to go on. Another woman recounted in a letter to her father how she had broken his favorite hairbrush while giving her son a spanking because the boy had disobeyed her twice in recent weeks.

GROWING UP IN SLAVERY

Less than one million Africans had been brought to these shores in chains when the slave trade ended in 1808. At the time of the 1860 census, only fifty-two years later, there were 3,952,760 slaves. More than half of these slaves were under the age of twenty.

Unlike fathers who were free, fathers who were slaves were not able to provide their children with housing, food, or clothing. That was done by the slave master, who had the final say over their lives. He could decide to break up a family at any time by selling one of its members.

FIGURE 1.9 *Slave family ties were strong even though slave marriages were not legally binding. This photograph, which was taken on a plantation near Beaufort, South Carolina in 1862, shows five generations of a slave family.*

(Timothy O'Sullivan, "Five Generations on Smith's Plantation, Beaufort," South Carolina, 1862. Library of Congress)

Knowing that they could be separated from their children, slave parents took care to teach their children to respect and depend on others in the slave community. Children called older slaves aunts and uncles whether or not they were kin, and they were taught to rely on their knowledge.

Because quick obedience could be a matter of life or death for them, slaves taught their children to obey unquestioningly any command given to them by whites or kinfolk by loudly ordering their children around, just as they themselves were ordered around by slave drivers. Most parents did not hesitate to whip their children when they disobeyed or got into mischief.

The center of the slave family was the mother. Often the father did not belong to the same master as the mother and could visit the family only on Sundays or when he could steal away for a few hours. While the mother was working, her young children were cared for by older children or by women too old to work in the fields.

On some plantations, children were separated from their mothers when they were still young. The abolitionist Frederick Douglass never knew who his father was, except that he was a white man. He was taken from his mother, who was a slave, when he was an infant. In his autobiography, he wrote, "I never saw my mother, to know her as such, more than four or five times in my life; and each of these times was very short in duration, and at night. . . . She died when I was about seven years old. . . . I was not allowed to be present during her illness, at her death, or burial. . . . Never having enjoyed . . . her soothing presence, her tender and watchful care, I received the tidings of her death with much the same emotions I should have probably felt at the death of a stranger."

Like other parents, slaves worried about their children's health and moral training, but their power to do anything for their children was limited. Jacob Stroyer, who had been a slave in South Carolina, recalled that when he was being trained as a jockey, his trainer often beat him. He asked his father to do something about it, but his father told him to work harder, "for I cannot do anything for you." When Jacob's mother tried to say something to the trainer, she was whipped. Caroline Hunter, who had been a slave in Virginia, recalled, "During slavery it seemed lak you'r chillun b'long to ev'body but you. Many a day my

THE SLAVE Narrative COLLECTION

During the Great Depression, the Federal Writers Project sent dozens of unemployed writers out to interview 2,300 former slaves in 1936–1938. The interviewers, who were mostly white, were told to write down the interviews as they were spoken. Many of the recollections in this book about what it was like to be a slave child come from *The Slave Narrative Collection*, which grew out of these interviews.

Some historians have criticized *The Slave Narrative Collection* because the interviews were conducted more than seventy years after slavery ended and the interviewees' memories of slavery were likely to have changed or faded. They have also criticized the language in the interviews, saying that many of the interviewers' transcriptions were influenced by stereotypes of how blacks speak. Even so, these interviews are valuable because they tell us something that we would have no other way of knowing — what it was like to be a young slave in the United States.

ole mama stood by an' watched massa beat us till dey bled an' she couldn' open her mouf."

Slaves still managed to participate in their children's lives even under difficult conditions. They tried to fill out the meager diet that the master gave their children with vegetables they raised on small garden plots and with meat or fish they obtained by hunting and fishing when they had the time. Fathers who had skills like carpentry or blacksmithing passed on those skills to their sons. Both parents did their best to give their children religious training. They also taught them songs and stories about their past.

Being a daughter, being a son

In all families, whether poor or rich, parents tried to prepare their sons and daughters for their roles as grown-up men and women. Parents taught both boys and girls to obey their elders, to be thrifty, to value hard work, to have self-control, and to feel affection for their family. Children were not supposed to show anger to their parents or to other family members. But boys were given much more freedom to be angry than girls. Parents encouraged their sons to be aggressive and competitive, but criti-

cized their daughters for the same kind of behavior. As their sons grew older, they allowed them more freedom to do as they liked.

Girls were more closely watched than boys. Parents expected their daughters to stop playing rough-and-tumble games and to start acting like "ladies" when they approached their mid-teens. Daughters were expected to be less selfish, less aggressive, less independent, and less physically active than their brothers. They were also expected to be more religious, spiritual, and moral than boys. "Oh that I could be a girl forever," one fifteen-year-old North Carolina girl wrote in her diary, as she looked back longingly on the days when she could run around with her brothers.

Daughters were almost always offered fewer educational opportunities than their brothers. In Daniel Drake's family, Daniel was sent to study medicine, while his sister Lizzie, who was two years younger, was kept at home to help with the housework and the younger children.

Girls today have many more opportunities to be educated and explore their interests than they did sixty or 160 years ago. In fact, more girls

SLEEPING ARRANGEMENTS

Has your mother ever ordered you to go to your room and stay there until she said you could come out? What your mother was taking for granted when she punished you this way was that you had a room to go to where you were alone. Two hundred years ago, few families could dream of such a luxury. Houses were small, with one or at most four rooms in which all indoor life — from being born to dying — took place within the hearing of other family members. There was no personal privacy. It was rare for children or anyone except parents to have their own rooms or even their own beds to sleep in.

Families fortunate enough to live in houses with more than one room usually used one for eating, indoor work, sitting, sleeping, and cooking. The second room, sometimes called the parlor, was used as the parents' bedroom and for entertaining on formal occasions. Children and other adults living in the household slept together in the hall or the loft — girls with girls and boys with boys.

This state of affairs gradually changed over the course of the nineteenth century as an increasing number of American families accumulated the money to build houses large enough to provide separate bedrooms for their teenage or grown unmarried sons and daughters.

FIGURE 1.10 *In the eighteenth and early nineteenth centuries, it was customary to dress boys and girls alike until they were about six years old. As infants, they wore long gowns. At about the age of three, they were put into short coats and half-length petticoats and pantaloons. Both sexes had their hair either cut short or in long curls.*

(Ambrose Andrews, *The Children of Nathan Starr*. The Metropolitan Museum of Art, Gift of Nina Howell Starr, in memory of Nathan Comfort Starr (1896–1981), 1987.)

attend and graduate from college today than do boys. But in general, parents still monitor their daughters more closely than they do their sons. In most North American families, girls are still raised to be less aggressive and independent and more generous and concerned about the feelings and well-being of others than their brothers. Girls are rarely given the same encouragement to participate in sports as boys are. And boys are still expected to express their anger more openly than are girls.

Modern parents may no longer demand total, unquestioning obedience from their children or expect them to never display their anger within the family circle as they once did, but they still try to teach their children to value hard work, to have self-control, and to feel affection for their family.

In An Orphanage

PITY THE CHILD

Julia Silverman (b. 1929)

When Julia Silverman was seven years old and her sister Lillian was nine, their father killed himself. Their mother could not pay their bills and was forced to close the little coffee shop she had run with her husband in San Francisco. She worked as a cook in a restaurant, but it was 1936, the middle of the Great Depression, and she could not make a living. The family's situation was desperate.

One Sunday morning, Julia, Lillian, and their mother dressed as if they were going on an outing. But instead of going to Fisherman's Wharf or Golden Gate Park or Playland as they often did on Sundays, they went to a place called Homewood Terrace — a family-style orphanage with two-story cottages. Because it was Sunday, many of the children who lived there were away visiting their relatives.

A silver-haired woman, who seemed to expect them, took them on a tour of the house; afterward they strolled around the grounds. Their mother asked the girls if they thought the place was nice. "You'll have fun playing with all the other kids," she told them. She bent down and drew them close to her.

The next thing Julia remembered was waking up in a strange, dark room. For the first time, she realized that her mother had left them alone in this place. Julia was scared. The place had so many rules that she was afraid she might break: Scrub the tub after you take a bath. Wash out your socks every night. Make your bed so there aren't any creases. Finish all the chores you are given. Stand when a grown-up comes into the room. If you rest your elbows on the dining table, an older kid can hit you with a knife handle. If you don't finish your food at mealtime, you have to sit in the dining room until you do, even if you are there all night. She heard that a kid who had wet his bed was made to wear the wet sheet the next day or be tied to the toilet.

> The next thing Julia remembered was waking up in a strange, dark room. For the first time, she realized that her mother had left them alone in this place.

Julia learned not to say much, and she began to have a strange, aching, hollow feeling in her chest. There was no one she could turn to. The older girls were mean to her. She felt safe only when she was alone.

Julia and Lillian did not talk about the way it was before. As far as Julia could tell, Lillian didn't talk to anyone. In fact, it seemed like nothing mattered to Lillian — even the fact that her hair had been cut off so that it stuck out behind her ears.

Mrs. Silverman wrote to her daughters, "My dearest babies, Be good, my babies, don't worry, don't be sad, my babies. I'm doing the best I can; we'll all be together soon." She wrote that she had found a job in a gold-mining camp in Alaska.

One day, after living in Homewood Terrace for almost two years, Julia and Lillian were taken to meet their mother at the Ferry Building in San Francisco. The girls thought they were going to Alaska. But instead, Mrs. Silverman left them at the Children's Home in Seattle.

Julia never heard anyone call her by her name at the Seattle Children's Home. She didn't know anyone else's name. She slept in a big dormitory with lots of other girls and ate in a dining room with long wooden tables. She washed a line of toilets every morning before breakfast. At mealtimes, she loaded the dishes into a dishwasher. She was always hungry because the food was terrible and there was never enough. The staff did not eat with the children. When she cleaned up the staff's plates after meals, Julia noticed that there were bits of egg and meat on them. The children were never given eggs or meat to eat. For dinner, they ate a piece of white bread with pale, thick gravy poured over it.

Julia Silverman
at age 9,
San Francisco, 1938.
(Julia Scully)

Julia didn't think about her mother or about Homewood Terrace. She didn't think about going to Alaska. She didn't cry. She didn't feel the hollow ache in her chest anymore. She felt as if she wasn't really there—as if she was encased in a glass cage and experiencing these things from a great distance.

Adapted from Julia Scully, Outside Passage.

SENT to the POORHOUSE

Anne Sullivan's mother died of tuberculosis in 1874 when Anne was eight years old. Two years later, her father disappeared, leaving her, her sister Mary, and her little brother Jimmy behind. Mary, who was healthy, was sent to live with an aunt. But no one in the family wanted the burden of caring for Anne, who was nearly blind from trachoma (an eye infection), or for five-year-old Jimmy, who had a tubercular growth the size of a teacup on his hip. So the two children were placed in the poorhouse at the State Infirmary in Tewksbury, Massachusetts.

Conditions at the poorhouse were unimaginably awful. Of the twenty-seven motherless babies who entered the place the same year as Anne and Jimmy, not one survived. Anne and Jimmy spent their first night there in a small room at the end of the ward, where corpses were put to wait for burial. Rats, mice, and cockroaches were everywhere.

Anne recalled that Jimmy used to tease the rats with long shreds of paper and shriek with delight when one of them leapt into the room and frightened the patients.

Jimmy died not long after they were sent to the poorhouse. After his death, Anne wanted to die, too. But Anne stayed at the almshouse for four years, living among unwed mothers and their children — many of whom were covered with syphilitic sores — and men who tried to molest her. In 1880, she was transferred to the Perkins Institution and the Massachusetts School for the Blind in Boston, where she was taught to spell and read braille.

It was through her connections at the school for the blind that Anne Sullivan was hired to care for a blind and deaf child named Helen Keller. Anne Sullivan became famous as the person who taught Helen Keller to speak, read, and write.

In an Orphanage

One of the worst nightmares you can have is that your parents have died or disappeared. What will happen to me? *you wonder.* Where will I go? What will I do? Who will take care of me? Will anybody love me? Will they understand how I feel? Or will they be mean?

For most children living in America today, that nightmare is just that — a bad dream — and the questions are ones that they will never need to have answered. But for many children living two hundred years ago, or even one hundred years ago, the nightmare of being orphaned was no dream and the question of what would become of them was urgent. We do not know how many children were orphaned before 1900, but in that year, nearly one quarter of all American children could expect to lose at least one of their parents before they reached the age of fifteen.

IN THE DAYS BEFORE ORPHANAGES

Although many children were orphaned before the 1820s, there were only a few orphanages in the United States. Orphaned children were usually sent to live with their relatives, and those who did not have any relatives to take them were sent to live in the district almshouse or poorhouse. In the almshouse, they lived with the homeless, the poor, the insane, the sick, and the disabled, as well as the town drunks and prostitutes. As late as 1910, according to the United States census, nearly twenty-five hundred children under the age of sixteen lived in almshouses — many of whom were born there.

Because local authorities never had enough money to care for these unfortunate people, conditions in almshouses were wretched. Disease and death were constant visitors there. Almshouse residents — including babies and small children — were given little to eat and only rags to wear. Although almshouse inmates were guilty of no crimes except being poor, they were given less food and poorer lodgings than criminals. In fact, according to an official report describing the conditions in New York state's almshouses in the 1850s, cows, horses, and dogs usually were better provided for.

Orphans over the age of seven did not stay in almshouses for long. Boys were usually apprenticed to farmers until they were twenty-one years old, while girls were sent to work as household servants until they were eighteen years old. People concerned with the welfare of orphans complained that the children were little better than slaves in these apprenticeships. They were not taught anything that would allow them to escape from a life of poverty when they became adults.

Poor widows with children or parents who were too sick to

HARPER'S WEEKLY.

JOURNAL OF CIVILIZATION.

Vol. XX.—No. 998.]   NEW YORK, SATURDAY, FEBRUARY 12, 1876.   [WITH A SUPPLEMENT. PRICE TEN CENTS.

Entered according to Act of Congress, in the Year 1876, by Harper & Brothers, in the Office of the Librarian of Congress, at Washington.

THE HEARTH-STONE OF THE POOR—WASTE STEAM NOT WASTED.—DRAWN BY SOL EYTINGE, JUN.—[SEE PAGE 131.]

work were sometimes given a kind of welfare called "outdoor relief." In Philadelphia in 1814, the average amount of money a family received for outdoor relief was seventy-seven cents a week. This was just enough money to keep a widow and her children from starving to death.

Some counties in New York, Rhode Island, New Hampshire, and other states auctioned off needy and orphaned children to the lowest bidder — the person who charged the county authorities the *least* amount of money to feed and house these children. The men who bid for the poor and orphaned children were not being charitable. They demanded work for the food and shelter they gave these children, and they tried to make a profit on top of that.

Orphans in orphanages

Given how badly orphaned children were treated in almshouses, it seems unbelievable that anyone would worry that the children would be spoiled and become dependent on the charity of others. But that is exactly what many reformers in the 1820s feared. They also worried that the drunks, prostitutes, and insane and feebleminded people who lived in almshouses

FIGURE 2.1 *This engraving from a February 12, 1876* Harper's Weekly *shows homeless children in New York City gathered around a steam grating to stay warm. Such scenes alarmed middle-class people, and orphanages were founded in response.*

(Sol Eytinge, Jr., *The hearth-stone of the poor — waste steam not wasted,* Harper's Weekly, February 12, 1876. The Library of Congress)

with the orphaned children were not setting a good example for them. They thought that taking orphaned children and placing them somewhere separate from grown-ups, where they could be taught to work and given religious training, would create independent, hardworking, God-fearing citizens. With this goal in mind, they began to found orphanages in the 1820s.

The people who founded orphanages wanted to rescue orphaned children — but not all orphans. Usually they worried about "their own kind" of children — European-American children who had the same religious background they did. Most orphan asylums founded in the nineteenth century were for white children. The vast majority of African-American children were slaves until 1863, and it was assumed that they were taken care of by their owners. After the Civil War, a few orphanages for African-American children were established, but by the early twentieth century, more than half of the charitable institutions for children in the United States still did not admit African-American children.

Like Julia Silverman, many of the children in orphanages had one living parent. They had been placed in an orphanage by their own mother or father. In some cases, parents paid the orphanage to care for their children until they found work or a better living

FIGURE 2.2 *In 1861, these children were photographed playing in front of the Colored Orphan Asylum in New York, which was one of the few orphanages for African American children before the Civil War. The orphanage was burned to the ground by a mob two years later during a riot.*

(Print Collection, New York Historical Society)

situation. Parents who placed their children in an orphanage lost control of them. The orphanages only permitted visits at specific times, and their children's letters to them were censored by the orphanage staff. If the orphanage suspected a poor parent of placing his or her children in their institution until the children were old enough to work, the orphanage might refuse to return the children when the parent came to reclaim them.

Placing children in an orphanage was hard for parents, but it was a thousand times harder for the children who were placed there. They were separated from everything they had ever known — home, family, friends, neighbors, and the familiar routines of their life. Sarah Sander recalled being brought to an orphan asylum in Cleveland with her sister Charlotte on a frosty night in January 1894, after her father died. Their clothes were taken away, and then they bathed in a pool of green water. In the changing room, "we put on a grey long-legged union suit of thick knitted material . . . which in the course of the day became a torture of itching; long black thick stockings, a red flannel 'underskirt' and a grey wool, ankle-length, long-sleeved dress — severely plain, and a blue-striped apron . . . My beloved patent-leather tipped, high buttoned shoes . . . were taken away

FIGURE 2.3 *This poor settler in Custer County, Nebraska lost his wife and was left with three small children to care for. Heavy rains had caused the roof of his sod house to collapse the night before this photograph was taken. Desperate situations like this one forced many parents to give up their children.*

(Solomon D. Butcher, "Three motherless children and a caved-in soddy", 1887, Nebraska State Historical Society Photograph Collections)

and I was given instead a pair of thick leather, red-lined, loose clodhoppers that fit nowhere and laced up over my ankles." Later that day, Sarah and Charlotte had their long hair cut off by a barber in the style of a boy's haircut. "I felt we had lost our identities," Sarah wrote.

Most orphanages were run like prisons. The children were awakened early in the morning by bells; called to meals, school, and work by bells; and then sent to bed by bells. They lived with dozens of other children in enormous rooms with row after row of narrow cots. They bathed in cold water. They were bullied and tormented by the older children. As if that weren't bad enough, they were sometimes beaten, kicked, and punched by the staff.

At the Cleveland orphan asylum where Sarah Sander was sent, the superintendent believed that military discipline was the only way to teach the children to be orderly, clean, and decent. Boys were beaten for bad behavior. Girls were not hit, but they were punished for breaking rules. Children who received twenty-one or more marks against them in a week were humiliated in front of all the other children. Any boy or girl caught leaving the building received one hundred marks against them and had to stay indoors for a week.

Food was a problem in almost every orphanage. In the Boston Female Asylum at the beginning of the nineteenth century, the children were given hasty puddings, boiled rice with molasses, or milk porridge for breakfast and supper. For dinner, they ate soup on Mondays and Wednesdays, boiled meat on Tuesdays, peas or beans with pork on Thursdays, mutton or lamb broth on Fridays, and fish on Saturdays. Sundays were only slightly better. One man recalled that when he was a child at the Cleveland Jewish Orphan Asylum, the portions were so small that it took the children about three minutes to finish eating.

The children would do just about anything to fill their stomachs. They stole food from the kitchen, bullied younger

FIGURE 2.4 In many orphanages, talking was forbidden during meals and at bedtime because the staff was afraid that the children would plan mischief or teach each other bad language and habits. These girls at the New York Foundling Hospital in 1900 sit facing the center of the room instead of one another.

("New York Foundling Hospital: Mealtime," 1900. Museum of the City of New York, Byron Collection)

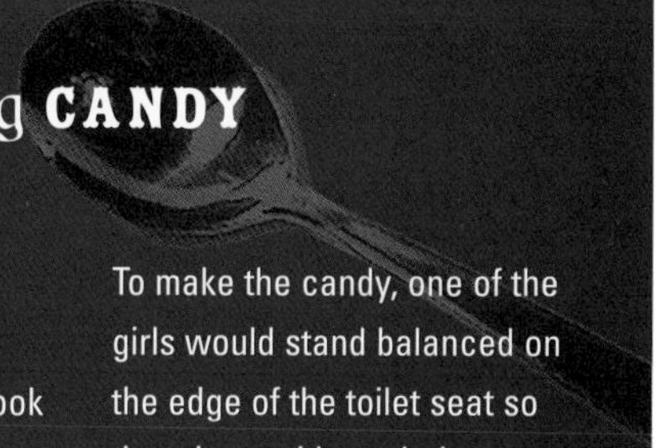

Making CANDY

Starved for sweets, the girls in the Cleveland Jewish Orphan Asylum took matters into their own hands and made candy in the girls' bathroom at night after the watchman had made his rounds. The ingredients for their candy making were simple — hoarded sugar from their morning cereal and the butter that was given to them with their baked potatoes. The plate and spoon they used were smuggled from the dining room in their bloomers.

To make the candy, one of the girls would stand balanced on the edge of the toilet seat so that she could reach the gas jet that was suspended from the ceiling. Like a doctor calling for his instruments, she would call to the other girls to hand her "the dish," "sugar," "butter," "the spoon." The girl would hold the plate over the gas jet with an outstretched arm and stir with the other hand, while another girl held on to her to keep her from falling. The "candy" was then put on the windowsill to cool before it was divided up and eaten.

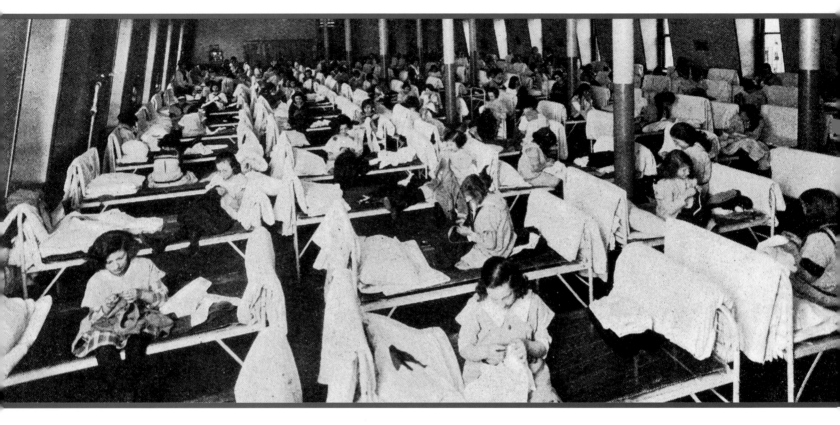

FIGURE 2.5 *Mending their own clothes was only one of the many tasks children in an orphanage had to perform to make the orphanage run smoothly.* (Underwood & Underwood, Hebrew Orphan Asylum, "Mending Time." Museum of the City of New York)

kids to get their meals, searched the trash for scraps they could eat, and snuck out of the orphanage to neighborhood shops or to the homes of their relatives to beg for or steal food.

Edward Dahlberg, who also lived in the Cleveland Jewish Orphan Asylum, recalled, "The fighters . . . would sneak out at night when the governors were at their meals, crawl over the transom of the bread-room and steal bread and apples." Sometimes they stole raw potatoes, which they roasted over a fire behind the playground. Another man at the same orphanage remembered climbing over the eight-foot fence that surrounded the orphanage with a gang of boys to go to a nearby bakery. Some of the boys would distract the baker

while others ran out with a tray of cakes.

Much of the day-to-day work in orphanages was done by the children. They also were required to spend several hours every day in the orphanage's workshops, where boys learned to carpenter, make shoes or baskets, or cane chairs and girls learned to embroider napkins and sheer handkerchiefs.

The education the orphans received was usually the most basic kind. Religious instruction taught them to fear God, be humble in the face of their problems, and be grateful for the care they received. In asylums that were supported by public taxes, the children were taught to be Protestants. Catholics and Jews were outraged by this practice and started their own

FIGURE 2.6 *These boys began their vocational training at the orphanage in which they lived at the age of eight. Here they are shown in a woodshop where they were taught carpentry.*

(Hebrew Sheltering Guardian Society: "Children State Vocational Training At the Age of Eight," Museum of the City of New York)

orphanages to keep Catholic and Jewish children from being converted to a Protestant faith.

SENT AWAY

By the 1850s, many people were beginning to complain that orphanages were too big, too cold, and too strict. One of the most influential of these critics was Charles Loring Brace, the director of the New York Children's Aid Society. He argued that children who were brought up in orphanages could not cope with real life after they were released into the world. He believed that the best place for a child to grow up was in a farm family.

Brace developed a program known as the "Orphan Trains." This program took hundreds of thousands of children from the streets and orphanages of New York and sent them on trains to live with farm families all over the United States. When the children arrived at their destination, the Children's Aid Society agent introduced each of them to the crowd of people interested in adopting them who had assembled at the local school, church, or community center. Applicants for children were then allowed to go up to the children and pick the one they wanted. If the boy or girl agreed, they went home with the person who chose them.

FIGURE 2.7 *These children on an Orphan Train in the nineteenth century were on their way to meet new families.*

(AT& SF Series, "Orphan Train," Kansas State Historical Society, Topeka, Kansas)

A boy or girl could refuse to go with the person who chose them if they wanted to. One man who had been on an orphan train recalled, "I refused to go home with two different farmers . . . but I was fortunate that I did not. The two boys the farmers adopted were hardly more than slaves to them. . . . Everyone seemed to think I was a very bad character and I was left alone on the stage that day, alone with no place to go. . . . A 60-year-old couple heard about me and . . . persuaded me to go home with them. . . . As it turned out, I had the best home of all the orphans I had come with."

The orphan trains were a happy solution for some children. "I went to school, church, and had as good a life as anyone around me. There seemed not to be anything different about my being an orphan," wrote a man who had been placed with a family in Arkansas as a boy. For others, the experience was not nearly as good. One man recalled that there had been no interaction with his new parents except for his work, his room, and his board. "They never touched me or said they loved me, and they didn't want me to call them Mom and Dad. Think what that does to you. They weren't mean, they were cold. . . . When I was fifteen or sixteen, I decided I'd live in a garbage can before I'd stay there any longer."

By the beginning of the twentieth century, there was a chorus of criticism directed at the orphan trains. Public officials

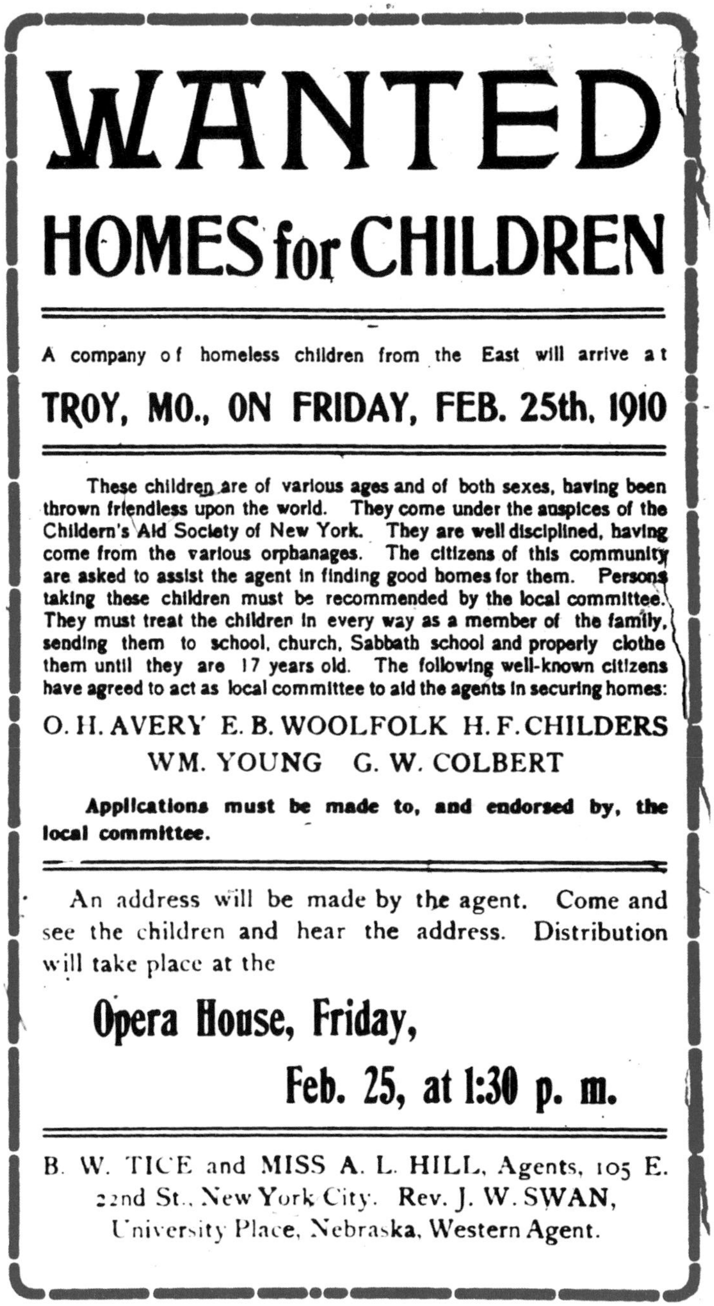

FIGURE 2.8 *This is a notice telling readers that a company of homeless children from the east will arrive in Troy, Missouri on February 10th, 1910. It says the children, who come from various orphanages, are well-disciplined and asks that the community help the agent place them into good homes.*

(Used by permission, State Historical Society of Missouri, Columbia)

WANTED
HOMES for CHILDREN

A company of homeless children from the East will arrive at

TROY, MO., ON FRIDAY, FEB. 25th, 1910

These children are of various ages and of both sexes, having been thrown friendless upon the world. They come under the auspices of the Childern's Aid Society of New York. They are well disciplined, having come from the various orphanages. The citizens of this community are asked to assist the agent in finding good homes for them. Persons taking these children must be recommended by the local committee. They must treat the children in every way as a member of the family, sending them to school, church, Sabbath school and properly clothe them until they are 17 years old. The following well-known citizens have agreed to act as local committee to aid the agents in securing homes:

O. H. AVERY E. B. WOOLFOLK H. F. CHILDERS
WM. YOUNG G. W. COLBERT

Applications must be made to, and endorsed by, the local committee.

An address will be made by the agent. Come and see the children and hear the address. Distribution will take place at the

Opera House, Friday,
Feb. 25, at 1:30 p. m.

B. W. TICE and MISS A. L. HILL, Agents, 105 E. 22nd St., New York City. Rev. J. W. SWAN, University Place, Nebraska, Western Agent.

in several states accused the Children's Aid Society of unloading juvenile delinquents on their states. People concerned with children's welfare condemned the society for not investigating the homes where the children were placed to see if they were suitable and for failing to follow up to see how the children were doing once they were placed. Catholics complained that Catholic children were being taken off the city streets and placed in Protestant homes so that they would become Protestants.

There was some truth to these charges, and they played a role in putting an end to the orphan trains. But the main reason was that the public's attitude toward child labor was changing. By the 1920s, when the orphan trains ended, many people no longer believed that it was good for children to work.

A number of new programs took the place of the orphan trains, including day care centers, grants for mothers that allowed working parents to keep their children, local foster care, and adoption.

Today there are few orphanages left in the United States. Children who are orphaned or whose parents cannot care for them are usually adopted right away or placed in foster care, or if they are teenagers, in group homes. Unfortunately, while the number of children who need foster homes continues to grow, good foster parents are in short supply. Our society has still not found a way to take care of all of its poor, abandoned, or orphaned children.

Turned Out DURING THE DEPRESSION

During the Great Depression of the 1930s, thousands of children like Julia Silverman were placed in orphanages by their families because they could not afford to feed them. Older children were sometimes turned out by their families and wandered around the country. Many other teenagers hit the road by choice when they realized that their families were broke.

Robert Chaney, who was one of ten children, was told by his father, "If I were a strong, healthy boy like you, I wouldn't hang around here and eat off my old man, I would go to California." Robert left home the next evening with a friend. His mother gave him a lunch bag filled with fried green tomatoes and some peanut butter sandwiches.

Tiny Boland left home when he was fourteen years old to look for work harvesting crops. "None of us knew anything about riding freight trains," he said. "You simply did it. You went down to the yards, climbed on a boxcar and went wherever the trains took you." By some estimates, as many as 250,000 teenagers wandered around the country during those hard years.

FIGURE 2.9 *This homeless boy is waiting for a place to spend the night at the city mission in Dubuque, Iowa. During the Great Depression, homeless teenagers slept in railroad cars, in hobo camps, or wherever they could find shelter.*

(John Vachon, Library of Congress)

A Child's PLEA

On her first evening in the orphan asylum, seven-year-old Charlotte Sander, Sarah Sander's sister, wrote this letter to her mother:

My dear Mother, it is not here as you thought — there is a big hall where all the children are — but I don't like to be here — I was crying and I want to go home — you must take me home — you must take me home — you must take me home — And Sarah — and they cut off my hair and they put on me such a long dress–but you must take me home. Sarah is very sick to see you and so am I. But please take Sarah and me home — if you don't take me home I will be sick — and I was crying when I wrote this letter.

In Sickness and in Health

SURVIVING AN EPIDEMIC

Ida Barnett Wells (1862–1931)

I t was the summer of 1878. Sixteen-year-old Ida Wells was visiting her grandmother when word came that there was a terrible outbreak of yellow fever in her hometown of Holly Springs, Mississippi. The entire population was moving out to the countryside to avoid catching the disease. Ida imagined that her parents had taken her sisters and brothers and left town like everyone else.

Not long after she heard of the epidemic, a call at her grandmother's gate brought news that changed her life. Three of her parents' friends were at the door, and one of them handed her a letter. "Jim and Lizzie Wells have both died of the fever," it read. Ida was stunned. Jim and Lizzie Wells were her father and mother.

Ida wanted to return to Holly Springs at once, but her grandmother, aunt, and uncle were not willing to let her go until they received a letter from the doctor there saying that it was safe for her to come. She left for the railroad station anyway. The people there argued that she would die if she returned home. At first, Ida reconsidered and started to go back to her grandmother's house, but when she thought of her sister Eugenia, who was crippled, and of her younger brothers and sisters, she returned to the station.

No passenger trains were running because of the epidemic, so Ida had to take a freight train. The caboose was draped in black because two conductors had recently died of the fever. The conductor told Ida that she was making a terrible mistake by going home. By way of a reply, Ida asked him why he was running the train when he was as likely to get yellow fever as the two conductors who had died. "Somebody has to do it," the conductor said.

"That's exactly why I am going home," she said. "I am the oldest of seven living children. There's nobody but me to look

While still a teenager,
Ida Wells took over the care of her
brothers and sisters
after the death of her parents.

(Library of Congress)

after them now. Don't you think I should do my duty, too?"

When Ida arrived home, she found two of the children in bed with yellow fever. Her nine-month-old baby brother had already died. Except for her sister Eugenia, all the other children had suffered mild cases of the disease. Ida developed a chill the day after she arrived. The old nurse who had been taking care of the children took no chances and put Ida to bed for four days and nights. She had Ida drink hot lemonade, which was the best remedy for fever anyone knew of at that time.

Ida's father had been a member of the Freemasons, an organization that cared for its members and their families in times of trouble. His Masonic brothers met at the Wellses' home on a Sunday afternoon after the epidemic was over to decide what should be done with the Wells children. After a long discussion, the men decided to give five-year-old Annie and two-year-old Lily to families who wanted the little girls. James and George would be apprenticed to men who would teach them carpentry. They would send Eugenia to the poorhouse because she had been left paralyzed by a previous illness and no one wanted her. Ida was old enough to look out for herself, they said.

When the men were finished talking, Ida calmly told them that they were not going to send any of the children anywhere. She would take care of them. But to do this, she needed their help finding work. The men scoffed at the idea of a sixteen-year-old girl taking care of so many children, but Ida refused to back down. In the end, they seemed to be relieved that she had taken the problem of caring for her family out of their hands.

Ida applied to teach in a school. After taking the examination, she was assigned to teach six miles from her home at a salary of twenty-five dollars a month. It was not practical for Ida to walk twelve miles every day, so she asked her seventy-year-old grandmother to stay with the children and help out during the week. Even after her grandmother suffered a stroke that left her paralyzed, Ida did not give up. She found a friend of her mother's to stay with the children during the week. Every Friday afternoon, she came home to spend Saturday and Sunday washing, ironing, and cooking for the children before going back to the school to teach on Monday morning.

For a young girl, Ida Wells showed remarkable courage in the face of illness and the loss of her parents. Her willingness to take on the responsibility of caring for her brothers and sisters after her parents died kept her family together for several years. With the high death rates that were common until the 1920s, many teenagers were faced with similar choices.

Adapted from Ida B. Wells, Crusade for Justice: The Autobiography of Ida B. Wells.

"I am the oldest of seven living children. There's nobody but me to look after them now. Don't you think I should do my duty, too?"

A Terrible PLAGUE

*Y*ellow fever killed thousands of people during the eighteenth and nineteenth centuries. Since no one understood what caused the disease, the best anyone could do when they heard that there was a yellow fever outbreak was to flee from it. In 1878, twenty-five thousand people left Memphis to avoid coming down with yellow fever. Today we know that yellow fever is caused by a virus that is carried by mosquitoes. There is no cure for the disease once it is contracted. Those who survive yellow fever usually develop an immunity to it. Vaccinations that give some protection against contracting the disease were developed in 1900.

In Sickness *and* in Health

To get an idea of just how risky life was for children growing up in the United States before the twentieth century, count yourself and all the other children you know. Then imagine that one out of every five of you died before you reached adulthood. Those are roughly the odds European-American children faced during much of the nineteenth century. The odds were much worse for Native American, Mexican-American, and African-American children.

Even as late as 1900, 140 babies out of every 1,000 born did not live long enough to see their first birthdays. Children were most often killed by diarrhea, dehydration, diphtheria, whooping cough, scarlet fever, measles, cholera, typhoid fever, pneumonia, tetanus, malaria, yellow fever, bronchitis, and influenza. Most died in their first year of life. In those days, people did not understand the nature of these diseases, how they spread, how to prevent them, or how to cure them.

THE BIGGEST KILLERS

The number one killer of babies was digestive problems, especially diarrhea and the dehydration that results from it. The next biggest killers of children were bronchitis, influenza, pneumonia, and a group of contagious diseases known as "childhood diseases." Thanks to preventive vaccinations and inoculations, many of the childhood diseases are rare in the United States today.

In the nineteenth century, diphtheria was one of the deadliest and most contagious of the childhood diseases. Diphtheria bacteria were passed through the air when infected children coughed or sneezed. Children could also catch the disease from touching something that an infected child had touched. Two or three days after being exposed to the bacteria, the child complained of feeling tired and having a headache, later developing a high fever, painful sore throat, and cough. As the child's air passages became coated with a thickening membrane, breathing became more and more difficult. Death usually came by suffocation. Between 30 and 50 percent of the children who contracted the disease died.

FIGURE 3.1 *Grave diggers in 1890 burying the tiny coffins of babies who died in New York City, many from diarrhea caused by drinking spoiled milk. They were buried three deep in unmarked graves. This isolated spot on Long Island Sound is still used as a burial ground for those who cannot afford a private burial.*

("Potters Field," Harts Island, Bronx, 1890, Museum of the City of New York, Jacob A. Riis Collection)

CURING THE SICK

What did mothers do when their children became sick? There were no special hospitals to take them to before 1855, and there were no doctors specializing in children's health until the 1860s. Mothers sent for a doctor if there was one nearby and they could afford to pay his fee. But many of them had no choice except to take care of their sick children themselves, especially when they lived on remote farms.

For advice on what to do to cure their child's cough or relieve their teething baby's fretfulness, mothers turned to books written by doctors. One popular book, written by Dr. William Dewees in 1838, recommended that calomel (a tasteless powder made from mercurous chloride) be given to babies suffering from diarrhea in "small but repeated" doses. For quieting the bowels at night, laudanum (a solution of opium in alcohol) enemas were prescribed. In cases of whooping cough (pertussis), Dr. Dewees advised mothers to apply leeches to the temples if the child's cough was accompanied by a headache. Leeches are bloodsucking worms that were used to bleed patients. They were a popular treatment for many diseases.

Medicines for various ailments could be bought from local drugstores (called apothecaries), from traveling salesmen, and through the mail. Many of the medicines available were of little value, and a few were downright harmful. Some

FIGURE 3.3 *Some parents never got over the death of a child. Here the Andrews family are at the grave of their son Willie, who died at the age of nineteen months on their ranch in Cedar Canyon, Nebraska.*

(Solomon Butcher, 1887, Nebraska State Historical Society, Photographic Collection)

FIGURE 3.4 *Before the twentieth century, it was not unusual for a family to experience the death of at least one of their children. Here a dead baby is lovingly laid out to be photographed before burial. In the late nineteenth century, many bereaved parents had their dead children photographed as a memento.*

(Kansas Collection, Pennell Collection, Kenneth Spencer Research Library, University of Kansas Libraries)

mothers made their own medicines from herbs and roots using family recipes or recipes they found in books like *The Indian Doctor's Dispensary, Being Father Smith's Advice Respecting Diseases and Their Cures.* The book recommended using plants to heal, such as Saint-John's-wort for the lungs and star root for sore throats. An application of corn snake root chewed until it became a soft, moist mass was recommended as a poultice for rattlesnake bites. For boils and other skin ailments, an application of the beaten bark of a white pine tree was recommended.

Some common home remedies — like rhubarb or powdered chalk mixed with gruel for diarrhea, a hot roasted onion applied to the ear for earaches, or a plaster of snuff applied to the chest for a hoarse, dry, hacking cough — may not have helped, but they also were not likely to do much harm. Other substances used to treat ailments, like mercury, opium, and quinine, were dangerous even in small amounts and may have been responsible for the deaths of some children.

TOO SAD TO BEAR

You would be making a mistake if you thought that it was any easier for parents to bear the death of a child in the nineteenth century than it is today. Children may have been more likely to die, but for their parents every loss of a child was a terrible one, never to be forgotten. Augusta Dodge, who lived in Kansas in the 1870s, recalled how her mother reacted when she saw that her twelve-year-old son was dead: "[H]er cry of agony was not human. Then it seemed as if she would never get her breath again." Her father stared, then started to shake and sob. The family spent several days with Augusta's grandparents after her brother's burial. When they walked back to their sod house, Augusta stopped in her tracks. The house wasn't there! Her father's grief was so desperate that he had pulled the logs from the roof, broken down the walls, and plowed over the ruins.

Terrible as it was, death was not treated as something that had to be hidden from sight. People died at home, and their families, including the children, were there to say goodbye and to witness their passing. Four-year-old Maria Foster was taken into the room where her dead father was laid out to say good-bye, even though she was sick. Years later, she still recalled touching his cold forehead.

William Dean Howells lived in southern Ohio in the 1840s. When his friend became sick from "the flux" (diarrhea), William recalled that, "On Friday, just before school let out, the teacher . . . rapped on his desk, and began to speak very solemnly. . . . He told us that our friend was lying very sick, so very sick that it was expected he would die; and then he read us a serious lesson about life and death, and tried to make us feel how passing and uncertain all things were so that we would resolve to live so that we never need be afraid to die.

"Some of the fellows cried, and the next day some of us went to see the dying boy. We were stricken when we saw our friend lying there white as the pillow with his blue eyes looking large and strange in his wasted face. The dying boy didn't say anything that we could hear, but he smiled and the light came into his eyes when his mother asked if he knew one or the other of us. It was too sad. We could not bear it and we went out of the room. In a few days we heard that our friend had died."

FILTH, POLLUTION, AND CROWDING

Even now, poor, slum-dwelling children are more likely to become sick than children who live in more comfortable

FIGURE 3.5 *Garbage collection services were overwhelmed in most cities throughout the nineteenth century and even in the first decades of the twentieth. Dead animals like this horse were left to rot on the street, spreading disease-causing flies and vermin.*

("The Close of a Career in New York," Byronic Photographic Firm, for Detroit Publishing Company. Library of Congress)

homes and neighborhoods. Diseases thrive and spread in damp, unventilated, poorly heated rooms where many people live crowded together. Between 1815 and 1914, crowding became a serious health issue. Many American cities were overwhelmed by a tidal wave of immigrants from the countryside and from Europe. To meet growing demand, housing was hastily built, creating slums. Even with these new buildings, housing shortages forced families to live crowded together, with many people in a single room.

New city services could not be put in place fast enough to meet the needs of the growing population. Sewage was dumped in nearby rivers that also provided the local water supply. Garbage was thrown onto unpaved streets, and dead animals were left to rot. Starving cats, dogs, and rats scavenged in the garbage that piled up in alleyways and backyards. Outhouses (a small structure with a wooden seat over a pit used as a toilet) were overused and poorly built so that they overflowed, causing raw sewage to run into the streets and water supply. In 1865, for example, the Cincinnati Board of Health reported that 102 people were living in a two-story tenement that had a single outhouse as its only toilet facility.

Conditions on the frontier were little better than in city slums. Most pioneer families lived crowded together in tightly packed houses where infections were likely to spread from one person to another. Infections also spread at social gatherings. In many frontier communities and mining camps, there were no sewers and the drinking water was contaminated by human and animal waste. As a result, many children died of cholera and other intestinal diseases.

Even as far back as 160 years ago, doctors and public health officials understood that poor sanitation and impure water were health hazards. They were alarmed by these filthy conditions and urged cities to build sewer and water systems and to improve sanitation. As a result of their efforts, beginning in the 1850s, many cities established programs that cleaned and paved city streets, removed garbage, and built water and sewage systems. These public health measures helped to prevent the spread of some diseases like cholera and typhus, which are carried by lice, ticks, and fleas, as well as yellow fever and malaria, which are spread by mosquitoes.

DON'T DRINK THAT MILK

Children today are urged to drink milk by their parents and their doctors. They are told, "It's good for you." But during the nineteenth century, the milk many city children were given to drink was *not* good for them. It gave many children diarrhea and killed thousands of babies. Before the 1930s, most families did not have refrigerators. Those families who could afford blocks of ice used them to cool their food. Those who could not afford ice had to buy their food in small quantities every day. Even then, the milk they bought spoiled easily in warm weather when bacteria quickly multiply.

Milk not only spoiled in the heat; it often was contaminated before it was even sold. Many cows had tuberculosis.

FIGURE 3.6 *To prevent babies from dying from diarrhea, milk stations were opened in poor neighborhoods in the 1890s during hot summer months when unrefrigerated milk spoiled quickly. Here poor families could buy clean, safe milk at a reduced price.*

("Penny Milk Station," 1917, Chicago Historical Society).

They were kept in filthy conditions where their udders and flanks were caked with mud and feces, which fell in the milk. Milk cans were unwashed and allowed to stand around without being cooled. To cover the taste of sour milk, some people who sold milk added sugar, molasses, chalk, and bicarbonate to the milk. To make the milk go further, they added water, which was often dirty and ünsafe to drink.

The realization that spoiled and impure milk was killing babies led several cities to pass laws in the 1880s forbidding the sale of watered-down or impure milk. By 1890, health departments in several cities were regularly sampling milk to make sure that it was pure.

Sewer systems, pure water and milk, and other public health regulations reduced the spread of disease and lowered the death rate. But these measures could not cure a person once they had a disease, nor could they get rid of a disease entirely. To do that required a better understanding of the causes of diseases and how to control them.

A NEW UNDERSTANDING OF THE CAUSES OF DISEASE

Until the 1880s (and even afterward), people believed that diseases were spread by miasmas — bad-smelling vapors that upset the body's delicate balance. To bring the body back into balance, one had to act on the body's blood, perspiration, vomit, urine, and feces. Doctors tried to cure their patients by purging them with powerful laxatives (like calomel), giving them strong substances to make them vomit, cutting their veins to make them bleed, applying bloodsucking leeches to their skin, putting strong substances on the skin to make it blister, or giving them hot drinks to make them sweat when they had a fever. Not surprisingly, many people died as a result of not just their illnesses but also the medicine used to help them.

The miasma theory of disease came under attack beginning in the 1860s, when the laboratory studies of Louis Pasteur in France, Robert Koch in Germany, and the clinical work of Joseph Lister showed that infectious diseases were caused by germs — microorganisms that could be seen only under a microscope. These discoveries led doctors to start washing their hands and sterilizing their instruments after meeting with each patient so that they did not spread diseases from one patient to the next. Pasteur invented a process that prevented microorganisms from growing in milk if the milk is heated to a high enough temperature to destroy bacteria and then cooled in sealed containers to avoid new contamination from the atmosphere. Once pasteurization became standard in the milk industry, the number of babies who died from digestive problems or dehydration brought on by diarrhea dropped sharply.

In 1882 and 1883, it was discovered that cholera and tuberculosis, two diseases responsible for the deaths of many children, were caused by microorganisms. By 1890, the germs causing diphtheria, pneumonia, and typhoid were identified. Soon after that, an antitoxin for diphtheria was developed that cured the disease if it was given within forty-eight hours of infection.

In those days, important scientific discoveries were still rare, and many doctors and scientists were slow to accept the idea that diseases are caused by tiny agents, called germs. After all, germs could not be seen except under a microscope. Besides, doctors who did accept the germ theory of disease could do little to cure the diseases caused by germs. Before sulfa drugs (antibacterial drugs derived from sulfonamide) became widely available in the late 1930s, and penicillin in the early 1940s, the best the medical profession could do to keep diseases from spreading was to isolate children with

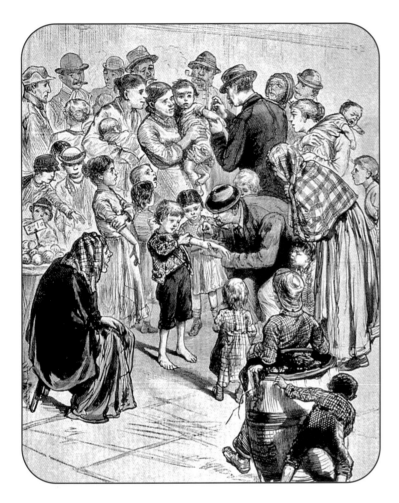

FIGURE 3.7 *Vaccinations for smallpox were developed in the late eighteenth century, but there were several outbreaks of the disease during the nineteenth century. Smallpox begins with flu-like symptoms of chills, high fever, nausea and aches. Within a few days, its victims develop an unsightly rash. The disease spreads easily from one person to the next by way of sneezing and coughing and contact with the scabs from the pustules or with the clothing of someone who has had the disease. It is estimated that smallpox has killed more people throughout history than any other disease.*

(Compulsory Vaccination in Jersey City — A Street Scene During the Smallpox Scare, Frank Leslie's Illustrated Newspaper, (November 19, 1881). National Library of Medicine)

infectious diseases and teach people to wash their hands, cover their noses and mouths when they coughed or sneezed, and handle food carefully. Thanks in large part to such preventive measures and to better living conditions, many fewer children were dying from such diseases as diphtheria and measles by the 1920s.

WATCH OUT! BE CAREFUL!

With fewer children dying from disease, public health officials and doctors turned their attention to preventing accidents, which even today are a major cause of death for children over the age of one. City streets were the playgrounds and living rooms for many children, especially those who lived in crowded apartments. The street was also where many children earned money by selling newspapers, shining shoes, or searching for things to sell. As horses and wagons gave way to cars, city streets became increasingly dangerous for children. In 1914, 60 percent of the traffic victims in New York City were children. Most accidents took place while children were playing or running errands near their homes. In response to these deaths, a "Safety First" movement aimed at children took shape in major cities, featuring widely publicized "Safety Days," "Safety Sundays," and "Safety Weeks." Safety became part of the school curriculum along with science, math, and spelling.

EXERCISE! IT'S GOOD FOR YOU

In the 1830s, Dr. John Gunn wrote, "If you would enjoy health, take *exercise* and be temperate; and . . . you will have little use for either physicians or medicines. . . . Persons who take proper exercise . . . are seldom sick." He maintained that a lack of exercise was responsible for such conditions as sleeplessness, constricted bowels, and dry, feverish skin. He

FIGURE 3.8 *This New York school for children suffering from tuberculosis — a bacterial disease that usually attacks the lungs — was operated in the open air because fresh air, rest and nourishing food were the best cure for the disease before modern drugs became available. The disease is spread from person to person through the air — often among family members or people who work or live together. In 1900, it was the second most common cause of death among adults and older children.*

("Organized Charity: Outdoor School," 1890. Museum of the City of New York, Jacob A. Riis Collection)

recommended a daily walk in the early morning air and an hour of exercise in the evening in the open air using weights.

Although Dr. Gunn's *Domestic Medicine* had a wide readership, his ideas regarding exercise were not popular with many girls in the middle of the nineteenth century. They thought exercise was boyish. It did not become fashionable for girls to participate in sports until the 1860s, when skating became the rage. It is a good guess that the reason for this change in the attitude of girls had nothing to do with the health benefits that come from exercise and everything to do with the discovery that you could have fun with others while you skated, practiced archery, played lawn tennis, or participated in any number of other sports.

It was all very well and good for children to exercise on their own after school, but many teachers believed that to remain alert in the classroom, children needed exercise during the school day, too. As a result, physical education became part of the school curriculum in many places. At the beginning of the twentieth century in the Chicago public schools, teachers led their classes in different exercises using beanbags, hoops, rings, four-foot-long poles, and Indian clubs, which were shaped like bowling pins. These exercises were not for fun. Rather, they were meant to strengthen muscles and improve agility and blood circulation. "It must be distinctly understood that school gymnastics are not recreation, they are school work," insisted the director of the Washington, D.C., program of physical training in a 1905 speech to the National Education Association.

EAT YOUR VEGETABLES!

When vitamins were discovered in the early twentieth century, doctors and other experts worried that children's diets did not provide them with the vitamins they needed. (Many children were fed a diet that was heavy on meats and sweets, with little in the way of vegetables or fruits.) To remedy this situation, doctors recommended that parents feed their children foods like carrots, spinach, and citrus fruits. Following this advice, many mothers refused to allow their children to leave the table until they finished their vegetables. They also forced their children to swallow a spoonful of bad-tasting cod-liver oil every morning so that they did not

develop rickets, a bone-deforming disease that is caused by a vitamin D deficiency. And for the same reason, they made their children drink several glasses of milk every day.

Despite all of the attention given to vitamin intake, diseases caused by vitamin deficiencies were actually rare in the United States — with the exception of pellagra, a disease caused by a lack of vitamin B_1, or niacin. In the early decades of the twentieth century, pellagra was most common among poor, rural families in the South who ate cornmeal rather than wheat bread.

FIGURE 3.9 *An outdoor stretching exercise using rods in 1899. Schoolchildren were also given "stretch and yawn," exercises during the school day as a way to relax their bodies and focus their minds.*

(Frances Benjamin Johnston, Library of Congress)

During the Great Depression of the 1930s, when millions of people had no work, many children did not have enough to eat. In 1937, President Franklin Delano Roosevelt said that one third of the nation was ill nourished and called for the federal government to ensure that people had a basic level of protection, including protection from hunger. Since that time, several laws have been passed to provide families with a basic safety net to prevent them from sinking into such poverty again. Nevertheless, the problem of hunger has not been solved for all American children. There are still hundreds of thousands of children in this country who go to bed hungry at night.

In the United States and in other developed countries, most of the diseases that killed children in the past have been brought under control. The most serious health problem facing many children today is neither disease nor hunger, but overeating. Thousands of American children face a lifetime of debilitating health problems because they are obese — they eat too much and they exercise too little. At the same time, in many places in the world, hunger and disease are still great scourges, killing thousands of children every year.

Being IMMUNIZED

These days one of the first shots American babies receive is called a DTaP shot — short for diphtheria, tetanus, and pertussis (whooping cough), all of which were big killers of children in the past. The shots work this way: Killed forms of the bacteria that cause these diseases are injected into babies. Their bodies react to the injection by forming antibodies against the bacteria. These antibodies give the children immunity to the diseases.

FIGURE 3.10 *Epidemics of poliomyelitis, a viral disease, were common in the summertime before the discovery of a vaccine in 1955. The disease can cause paralysis of the muscles. When the lung muscles are paralyzed, the victim dies or must live with artificial help in breathing. Children who survived polio often ended up with crippled legs. Like the boy pictured here, they needed leg braces and crutches to walk.*

(Roy Perry, "Polio Victim," Association for Aid to Crippled Children, Museum of the City of New York)

At Work
Earning her Keep

Rose Gollup (1880—1925)

In the winter of 1891, Rose Gollup's father fled from the oppression and poverty of Russia. He came to America, hoping to find a better life for himself and his family. He left Rose, her mother, and the other children behind until he could earn enough money to pay for them to join him. A year and a half later, he sent the family a package containing two steamship tickets to America — one for Rose, who was twelve, and the other for her aunt, who was twenty-one years old.

49

Rose arrived in New York on July 1, 1892. A little more than a week later, Rose's father put her to work. He had taught her to sew as soon as she was old enough to hold a needle, and he knew that she would have no trouble finding work in one of the many sweatshops in New York's Lower East Side. He needed Rose's help to save enough money to bring over the others in the family.

Rose's father was a coat finisher who was paid by the coat. As soon as Rose learned how to baste pocket flaps, her father began to teach her to baste the coat edges. They were thick, and Rose's fingers stiffened in pain as she rolled and basted the edges. When her father saw her struggling to finish an edge, he would offer to do it for her, but she wouldn't let him. She wanted to learn to do it herself.

It was not long before Rose's father decided that Rose knew enough to get a job of her own. He found work for her in a shop making overcoats. Her first morning she wrapped her thimble and scissors, along with a piece of bread for breakfast, in a bit of newspaper and stuck two needles in her coat lapel before she started off. Rose wrote in her autobiography about her first two days at work in the shop: "A tall, dark beardless man stood folding coats at a table. . . . I said, 'I am the new fellerhand.' He looked at me from head to foot. . . .

"'It is more likely,' he said, 'that you can pull bastings than fell sleeve linings. . . . Let's see what you can do.' He kicked a chair, from which the back had been broken off, to the finisher's table, threw a coat upon it. . . .

"All at once the thought came: 'If I don't do this coat quickly and well he will send me away at once.' I picked up the coat, threaded my needle, and began hastily, repeating the lessons father impressed on me. 'Be careful not to twist the sleeve lining, take small false stitches.'

"My hands trembled so that I could not hold the needle properly. It took me a long while to do the coat. But at last it was done. I took it over to the boss and stood at the table waiting while he was examining it. He took long, trying every stitch with his needle. Finally he put it down and without looking at me gave me two other coats. I felt happy! . . .

"All day I took my finished work and laid it on the boss's table. He would glance at the clock and give me other work. Before the day was over I knew that this was a 'piecework shop' . . . I also knew that I had done almost as much work as 'the grown-up girls' and that they did not like me. I heard Betsy, the head feller hand, talking about 'a snip of a girl coming and taking the very bread out of your mouth.'

"Seven o'clock came and every one worked on. I wanted to rise as father had told me to do and go home. But I had not the courage to stand up alone. I kept putting off going from minute to minute. My neck felt stiff and my back ached. . . . When the people began to go home it seemed to me that it had been night a long time.

"The next morning when I came into the shop at seven o'clock, I saw at once that all the people were there and working as steadily as if they had been at work a long time. . . . [T]he boss shouted gruffly, 'Look here, girl, if you want to work here you better come in early. . . .' He brought me two coats and snapped, 'Hurry with these!'

Rose Gollup in 1920, at the time
her memoir was published.
(Thomas Dublin and Amy Hyman)

"From this hour a hard life began for me. He refused to employ me except by the week. He paid me three dollars and for this he hurried me from early until late . . . but he was never satisfied. By looks and manner he made me feel that I was not doing enough. Late at night, when the people would stand up and begin to fold their work away and I too would rise feeling stiff in every limb and thinking with dread of our cold empty little room and the uncooked rice, he would come over with still another coat.

"'I need it the first thing in the morning,' he would give as an excuse. I understood that he was taking advantage of me because I was a child. And now it was dark in the shop except for the low single gas jet over my table and the one over his at the other end of the room . . . more tears fell on the sleeve lining as I bent over it than there were stitches in it. . . .

"[When I came home] Father explained, 'It pays him better to employ you by the week. Don't you see if you did piece work he would have to pay you as much as he pays a woman piece worker? But this way he gets almost as much work out of you for half the amount a woman is paid.'

"I myself did not want to leave the shop. . . . To lose half a dollar meant that it would take so much longer before mother and the children would come. . . . I longed for my mother and a home where it would be light and warm and she would be waiting when we came from work. . . . I pictured myself walking into the house. There was a delicious warm smell of cooked food. Mother greeted me near the door and the children gathered about me shouting. . . . I used to keep this up until I turned the key in the door and opened it and stood facing the dark, cold, silent room."

It took almost a year for Rose and her father to save up enough money to pay for her mother and the younger children to come to New York. A few months after Rose's family was reunited, work became scarce. Rose's father went out to look for work every day, but there was none to be found. When a woman they knew suggested that Rose take a job as a servant, her mother refused, saying, "Is this what I have come to America for, that my children should become servants?" But when their last cent was gone and her mother could not pay the coal man or the grocer, she was forced to let Rose take the job.

Rose did not mind working as a servant because she wanted to help her family and she wanted to know how people with money lived. Rose had to carry the coal from the cellar and light the fire every day. She had to wash and iron the clothes, scrub the floors, scale fish, clean chickens, make noodles, and run to the store whenever her mistress asked her to. The family she worked for slept in beds, but Rose was given two chairs to sleep on and some dirty quilts with which to cover herself. The mistress of the house carefully doled out Rose's food, giving her the least desirable parts to eat — the gizzards of the chicken, the tail of the fish, and the apples with brown spots. On Saturday nights, when the family had tea and cake, Rose was sent to bed with nothing to eat.

After working as a maid for two months, Rose quit. She decided that even if she had been forced to work hard in the shop, it was better than working as a servant. In the shop, she was not alone. She was a worker among other workers. And she could go home in the evening to be with her family.

Rose continued to work in sweatshops and clothing factories. Eventually she married Joseph Cohen. After their daughter was born, Rose stopped working and took writing classes. She wrote *Out of the Shadow*, a book about her life that has become a classic account of immigrant life in the Lower East Side of New York at the end of the nineteenth century.

Adapted from Rose Cohen, Out of the Shadow.

CHAPTER FOUR

At Work

Rose Gollup's father was not being cruel to Rose when he sent her to work in a sweatshop when she was only twelve years old. He was just doing what other parents did when they needed money. Children had always worked. They worked everywhere — on farms; in factories, mines, shops, and stores; in their own homes and other people's houses; as well as on the streets selling and scavenging. Many children who lived in New York's Lower East Side in the 1890s worked to help support their families.

Everyone believed that work was good for children. It keeps them busy and out of trouble and it prepares them for grown-up life. But most children did not work because people said it was good for them or because they were preparing for grown-up life. Like Rose Gollup, they worked because their families could not get along without their help. The money that they earned belonged to their parents, who could spend it any way they wanted to, as long as the children were living with them. (Even today, parents can legally claim their child's wages if they wish to.)

By the end of the nineteenth century, many city children were rebelling against the practice of handing over their pay envelopes to their parents unopened. They wanted money to spend as they saw fit — whether it was on a new dress, a game of pool, cigarettes, or a movie. Instead of waiting for their parents to decide how much money to give them out of their pay envelopes, they took a dollar or two for themselves before they reached home. Parents may have suspected that their children were holding out on them, but there was not much they could do about it. They were afraid that if they punished them, their children might move out, and then the family would not get any of their pay. Often the only solution was to compromise and permit children to take a few dollars out of their pay envelopes.

While some children resented being put to work, most took it as a matter of course. Some were happy to be able to help their families. Lucy Larcom, who went to work in a cotton mill in 1835 when she was eleven and a half years old, recalled, "I thought it would be a pleasure to feel I was not a trouble or burden or expense to anybody. So I went to my first day's work in the mill with a light heart."

ON THE FARM AND IN THE COUNTRYSIDE

On farms two hundred years ago, everyone worked, even little
children. They began helping their parents when they were little more than five years old. They gathered the kindling for the
fire, brought the water from the spring or well house, fed the
pigs and chickens, gathered eggs, and picked berries and nuts
in the woods.

By the time they were seven or eight years old, boys (and
sometimes girls) were herding cows and sheep. Like Daniel
Drake, they helped to guide the oxen when their fathers were
plowing. Afterward they used knives and hoes to break up the
big clods of dirt that were left behind the plow. Plowing, which
required a lot of strength, was usually reserved for grown men,
but sometimes boys were given the job. Hamlin Garland lived

on a farm in Minnesota in the 1870s, and he was just ten years
old the first time he plowed by himself. "I drove my horses into
the field that first morning with a manly pride. . . . I was grown
up!" he recalled. But his excitement soon came up against real-
ity: "To guide a team for a few minutes as an experiment was one
thing — to plow all day like a hired hand was another. It was not
a chore, it was a job. It meant moving to and fro hour after hour,
day after day, with no one to talk to but the horses. It meant
trudging eight or nine miles in the forenoon and as many more
in the afternoon, with less than an hour off at noon."

FIGURE 4.2 *Alice Butcher may have only been posing for her father when he took this picture of her milking a cow in Middle Loup Valley, Nebraska around 1905. But in many farm families, it was a girl's job to milk the cows at daybreak and again in the evening. It was also the job of the girls in the family to churn butter and make cheese.*

(Solomon Butcher, Nebraska State Historical Society, Photographic Collection)

Boys dropped the seed into the furrows created by the plow and covered them over with soil. They hoed and pulled the weeds that were crowding out the crops. The job of chasing away the birds and animals that threatened to devour the tender green shoots fell to them. At harvesttime when the crops had to be brought in, boys joined their parents to work long, backbreaking days. They raised cows, pigs, and sheep, which they helped their fathers to butcher. They also hunted and fished, both for fun and to put food on the table.

Girls worked just as hard as their brothers did. When they were as young as six, they took charge of their younger brothers and sisters and kept them from getting underfoot when their parents were working. They carded wool so it could be spun into yarn, and they helped with the cleaning, cooking, and weeding.

Maria Foster Brown, who lived in Athens, Ohio, in the 1830s, told her granddaughter: "Ma put us girls to work early. It was taken as a matter of course that we should learn all kinds of housework. I know that before I was seven years old I used to wash the dishes. Sister Libbie and I usually did the washing. . . . There was need of many hands to get all the work done. It required more knowledge to do the things for everyday living than is the case nowadays. If one wants light now, all one has to do is pull a string or push a button. Then, we had to pick a coal with tongs, hold it against a candle, and blow. And had to make the candles. . . .

"Even without candle making, there was certainly a plenty to do to keep life going in those days. Baking, washing, ironing, sewing kept us busy. Not to mention the spinning and weaving that had be done before cloth was available for the seamstress."

This way of life gradually began to give way in the Northeast as families turned from farming to trade and manufacturing, and in the Midwest where farms became mechanized. But it continued for another hundred years in many parts of the rural South, as well as on poor prairie farms and ranches in the West.

DOUBLE DUTY

While most children worked to help their own families, enslaved children were expected to work for their masters. When they were too small to work in the fields, they were given chores to do around the plantation. Little girls dusted, polished silver, set the table at the big house, helped the cook, and watched the master's younger children. With their brothers, they gathered firewood. Young boys tended sheep, milked cows, and toted water out to the fields for the field hands to drink and to the big house for cooking, cleaning, and washing. Henry James, who grew up in Virginia before the Civil War, "[u]sed to pack water to twenty-five and thirty men in one field, den go back to de house and bring enough water for breakfast de next morning." Children were also put to work sweeping the yard, guiding the oxen when the fields were plowed, and running errands. And after doing all of these things for the master, they then had to do many of the same things, like gathering firewood or tending kitchen gardens, for their own families.

Sometime between the ages of five and ten, slaves were taken out into the fields to hoe weeds or help their parents at harvesttime. Mary Reynolds, who had been a slave as a child, recalled that she had a hard time learning how to handle her hoe when she was first being taught how to "scrape the fields." She told an interviewer in the 1930s, "That old woman would be frantic. She'd show me and then turn 'bout to show some other little nigger, and I'd have the young corn cut clean as grass. She say, 'For the love of God, you better larn it right, or

FIGURE 4.3 *Entire sharecropping families, including children, worked to bring in the cotton harvest. On cotton plantations, the smallest children were given the job of picking the first balls of cotton from the lower part of the stalk.*

(From the stereographic collection of the New York Historical Society)

Cotton is King, Plantation Scene, Georgia, U. S. A.
Copyright, 1895, by Strohmeyer & Wyman.

Solomon will beat the breath out you body.' Old Man Solomon was the nigger driver."

On tobacco farms in the days before insecticides, children were given the chore of picking the worms off the plants. Some overseers forced the children to eat any of the worms they missed so that they would be more careful in the future.

On many plantations, there was a direct connection between how much food a slave was given and how much work he or she was able to do. Children beginning to work in the fields were called "quarter hands" and were given a quarter of the rations of a fully grown, skilled field hand, who was called a "full hand." If children wanted more to eat, they had to get it themselves by hunting, fishing, or gathering food from the woods. They also got food from their families, who grew it in the time they had left over after working for the master. Needless to say, they often had to go hungry.

Even after slavery was abolished, many African-American families were so poor that their children were forced to work as hard as they had ever worked under slavery, if not harder. When slavery ended, former slave owners divided up their land into plots, which they gave to black families to farm in exchange for a share of their harvest. Sharecropping families did not have

WHAT'S in a Name?

From its very beginning, America has been a country of immigrants who came from different parts of the world, bringing with them their own customs, religions, and languages. These immigrants have made the United States one of the most diverse countries in the world. But these different groups have always competed against one another for land, labor, and political power. Often this competition has led to bad feelings, with one group of people thinking that they are better than another group. One way that these attitudes have been expressed is in the names people have called one another.

The names change with the times. People whom we used to call "Indians" (because Christopher Columbus mistakenly believed he had sailed to India) are now called Native Americans. People from Mexico, Central America, and parts of the Caribbean are called different names in different parts of the country. "Hispanic," "Latino," "Chicano," and "Mexican" are all used, but not all are equally acceptable to the people who are called those names.

Most troublesome have been the names that have been used for the people who came from Africa as slaves. In the early history of the United States, they were called "Negroes," which came from the Spanish and Portuguese terms for "black." But European Americans sometimes used the word "nigger" as a way of expressing their feelings of superiority to the people who were their slaves. Sometimes African Americans used the word "nigger" too, but then it had another meaning. Later, the word "colored" came into use and was considered a polite term, and although it is no longer, the phrase "people of color" is considered acceptable.

In the 1960s, the people who traced their ancestry back to Africa began calling themselves "black" as a matter of pride. Today "black" and "African American" are the usual names that these people are called. It is considered insulting to call a person a "nigger." The one exception to this rule is when African Americans call each other "nigger," in circumstances that signal that they recognize they are often discriminated against.

In reading this book, it is important to keep in mind these changes in what groups of people are called. There are times when a person who is being quoted will refer to someone else in ways that were common at the time but which we consider inappropriate now. And sometimes those names — like "nigger" or "Meskins" — were rude even at that time.

enough money to buy farm machinery, so they had to do the work themselves. Even with their children working alongside them in the fields, they had a hard time earning enough money to keep going after they gave a share of their crop to their former master. To bring in more money, families often arranged for their sons to be hired as laborers in the slow season on the farm. Girls stayed behind with their mothers and worked for white families cleaning and doing laundry.

LEARNING ON THE JOB

Not every boy or girl was destined to farm. In the eighteenth and early nineteenth centuries boys whose fathers were tradesmen or skilled workers often became apprentices. Many others left their families to go to town to learn a trade. They entered into a legally binding agreement, called an apprenticeship, in which they worked for a master craftsman and learned his trade — be it sailmaking, printing, bricklaying, or blacksmithing — while the master craftsman gave them food, a place to sleep, and a small allowance, in addition to teaching them to read, write, and do simple arithmetic. Apprenticeships traditionally lasted from the time a boy was fourteen until he was twenty-one years old,

FIGURE 4.4 *In this engraving of an early nineteenth century printing office, a man is setting type while another man and an apprentice are working the press. When Horace Greeley was an apprentice, he was paid $40 a year and given some additional money for clothing in exchange for his work.*

(Edward Hazen, *The Panorama of Professions and Trades*, Philadelphia: Uriah Hunt, 1836. B21605, Old Sturbridge Village)

although many apprenticeships were becoming shorter by the beginning of the nineteenth century. At the end of the apprenticeship, the young man was given a suit of clothes, a small sum of money, and the freedom to leave his master to go out to work on his own as a journeyman.

In 1826, at the age of fifteen, Horace Greeley was apprenticed to a printer in East Poultney, Vermont. Once his father and the printer agreed on the terms of Horace's apprenticeship, Horace went straight to the printing office and took his first lesson in the art of setting type. As the new boy in the shop, he was subject to hazing by the other apprentices. They threw type at him and spoke rudely to him, but he did not answer them. The oldest apprentices even applied ink to his blond hair while the journeymen, the pressmen, and the editor watched in silence. Horace kept on working as if nothing had happened. After trying to have their fun with him, the other apprentices gave up teasing Horace. Three days later, they were all friends.

Girls were apprenticed, too, though much less often than boys because most trades were closed to women. Sometimes girls were apprenticed to milliners and seamstresses to learn to make hats and clothes. Usually they were sent to work as servants when they were apprenticed.

Apprenticeship arrangements began to break down in the early nineteenth century as the country became increasingly industrialized. Children continued to be apprenticed to learn trades like bricklaying, sailmaking, and printing, though much less frequently than before as new industries and ways of doing things replaced the old. Master craftsmen no longer always promised to educate and clothe their apprentices. For their part, apprentices began to look for work on their own before they were finished with their apprenticeships. They were hired as helpers by other craftsmen because they would work for less money than trained journeymen who had finished their apprenticeships. And even as apprenticeship was disappearing from many trades, it was still used as a way of caring for orphans or older children whose families were too poor to care for them. The children were usually apprenticed to farmers, where they earned their keep by working as farm laborers if they were boys, or servants if they were girls.

Apprenticeship still exists, but it is very different than it was two hundred years ago. Modern-day electricians, tool and die makers, cabinetmakers, and many other skilled craftsmen learn their trades by serving apprenticeships under master craftsmen. Most young men and women enter apprenticeships through union, industry, or junior college–sponsored training programs, and they are not bound by any contract.

IN THE MILL

If a child didn't work on the farm in the nineteenth century, chances are he or she worked in a mill. Thousands of children did. They were among the first employees in the textile industry. Textile mills valued child employees because they were quick and they had good manual dexterity, but above all because they could be paid less than adults.

The first cotton mill in the United States was founded in 1790 in Pawtucket, Rhode Island, by Samuel Slater, who learned from the English the secret of using water power to drive machinery that spun cotton into yarn. Among Slater's first employees were nine children between the ages of seven and twelve. Slater advertised in newspapers and circulars for families with five or six children to come work for him. Although no one had ever worked in a cotton mill like Slater's before, people were used to working in family groups on their farms. Ten years later, there were one hundred children working in Slater's mill. The youngest was four years old.

It was the children's task to spread cleaned cotton onto a machine to be combed. Then they would pass on the combed cotton to other children who operated a machine that turned the cotton into loose balls. The cotton balls were then passed to more children who operated a machine that spun the cotton into yarn.

Because heat and moisture helped to keep the cotton threads from breaking, the windows in cotton mills were kept closed. The steamy air was filled with floating lint that got into the children's eyes and lungs and made them sick. The noise from the grinding of the gears of the machinery and the banging of the wooden frames was deafening. The moving machinery was open and unprotected. If the children weren't careful, they could fall into it or be caught by it. Children sometimes lost fingers or had their hands mangled by the machinery.

In 1793, only a few years after Slater built his mill that allowed water-driven machines to spin cotton, Eli Whitney invented a device called the cotton gin (short for engine) that

FIGURE 4.5 *In 1913, this girl worked as a spinner in a New England cotton mill to earn her keep. Like other mill and factory workers, she worked from 5:30 in the morning until 7:30 in the evening, with only two short breaks to eat.*

(Lewis W. Hine "Spinner in New England Mill," 1913, Courtesy George Eastman House)

WORK IN
Native American
FAMILIES

Native American children were also expected to help their families. "My mothers began to teach me household tasks when I was about twelve years old," Waheenee, a Hidatsa woman born in the 1840s, recalled. Her first task was to fetch water from the river. After that she learned to cook, sweep, and sew with an awl and sinew. She was taught to embroider with quills. She was also called upon to help with the harder work like gathering wood, dressing and scraping animal hides, and working in the family's cornfield.

Geronimo, the Apache warrior, also recalled being made to work as a child: "[W]e went to the field with our parents: not to play but to toil." At around the age of eight, he was taught to hunt on horseback and to stalk deer on foot.

let a man and a horse clean the seeds from cotton fifty times faster than it could be done by hand. Soon red-brick textile mills were springing up along New England's swift-moving rivers. There was huge demand for women and children to work in these mills.

In 1835, when she was only ten years old, Harriet Hanson went to work in a cotton mill in Lowell, Massachusetts. "I worked first in the spinning-room as a doffer. . . . I can see myself now, racing down the alley, between the spinning frames, carrying in front of me a bobbin box bigger than I was. These mites had to be very swift in their movements, so as not to keep the spinning-frames stopped long, and they worked only about fifteen minutes in every hour. . . . The working-hours of all girls extended from five o'clock in the morning until seven in the evening with one-half hour for breakfast and for dinner. Even the doffers were forced to be on duty nearly fourteen hours a day and this was the greatest hardship in the lives of these children. . . ."

Exhausted by working fourteen hours a day, five and a half days a week, children fell asleep at the machines. When the overseers found them, they were rudely awakened and sometimes beaten. The doffers would sometimes get into trouble when they would pass the time between changing bobbins playing around the spinning frames, "teasing and talking to the older girls, or entertaining [themselves] with games and stories in a cor-

ner." When the boys who swept up and did other work fooled around, the overseer threatened them and sometimes whipped them.

In 1836, the Lowell mills cut the workers' pay and did away with their twenty-five cent food allowance. To protest these cuts, the workers called for a strike. Harriet Hanson, who was eleven and a half years old, remembered that the girls she worked with were scared and could not decide whether to join the protest or not. Becoming impatient with their talk, she said, "'I don't care what you do, I am going to turn out whether any one else does or not,' and I marched out and was followed by the others."

The strike failed and the ring leaders were punished. Because of Harriet's participation in the strike, her mother was no longer allowed to run her boardinghouse for girls who worked in the mill, which is how she had earned her living.

More than twenty-five thousand children under the age of fifteen were working in cotton mills in 1925, when the drive to end child labor was in full swing.

IN THE MINES

In the days before electric power and combustion engines, coal was used not only to heat homes but also to fuel trains, steamships, and factories. As the United States became industrialized, the demand for coal grew, and with it, the demand for children to work in the coal

[1870]

75 Young Women

From 15 to 35 Years of Age,

WANTED TO WORK IN THE

COTTON MILLS!

IN LOWELL AND CHICOPEE, MASS.

I am authorized by the Agents of said Mills to make the following proposition to persons suitable for their work, viz:—They will be paid $1.00 per week, and board, for the first month. It is presumed they will then be able to go to work at job prices. They will be considered as engaged for one year, cases of sickness excepted. I will pay the expenses of those who have not the means to pay for themselves, and the girls will pay it to the Company by their first labor. All that remain in the employ of the Company eighteen months will have the amount of their expenses to the Mills refunded to them. They will be properly cared for in sickness. It is hoped that none will go except those whose circumstances will admit of their staying at least one year. None but active and healthy girls will be engaged for this work, as it would not be advisable for either the girls or the Company.

I shall be at the Howard Hotel, Burlington, on Monday, July 25th ; at Farnham's, St Albans, Tuesday forenoon, 26th, at Keyse's, Swanton, in the afternoon; at the Massachusetts' House, Rouses Point, on Wednesday, the 27th, to engage girls,---such as would like a place in the Mills would do well to improve the present opportunity, as new hands will not be wanted late in the season. I shall start with my Company, for the Mills, on Friday morning, the 29th inst., from Rouses Point, at 6 o'clock. Such as do not have an opportunity to see me at the above places, can take the cars and go with me the same as though I had engaged them.

I will be responsible for the safety of all baggage that is marked in care of I. M. BOYNTON, and delivered to my charge.

I. M. BOYNTON,

Agent for Procuring Help for the Mills.

FIGURE 4.6 *The girls who answered this ad signed up to work in a mill for one year at wages of one dollar a week.*

("75 Young Women . . . Wanted," Baker Library, Harvard Business School)

industry. By the end of the nineteenth century, thousands of fourteen- and fifteen-year-old boys worked belowground. Thousands more worked outside the mines in the coal breakers.

The coal breaker was a tall structure, four or more stories high, where coal was broken down and sorted. Then it was sent sliding down long chutes, spewing black clouds of coal dust that settled over boys who sat on planks nailed across the chutes. It was the breaker boys' job to pick through the coal and take out any pieces of slate, rock, or trash that would not burn. To keep from breathing in the coal dust, the boys wore handkerchiefs over their mouths, and they chewed tobacco to keep their mouths from drying out.

The boys sat hunched over the coal ten or eleven hours a day with only a short lunch period. It was backbreaking, growth-stunting, life-shortening work. The coal dust they breathed was so thick there were times when they needed miner's lamps on their heads to see. Many of the boys suffered from coughs that caused them lifelong health problems. The boys were not allowed to wear gloves on the job because gloves interfered with their ability to pick out the slate. Until their fingers were hardened, their skin was irritated by the sulfur on the coal and their hands swelled, cracked open, and bled. The sharp rocks cut their fingers. Sometimes if a boy reached too far, he might slip into the coal moving beneath him and be crushed to death.

ON THE CITY STREETS

Many immigrant children earned their first pennies in the new country sitting around the table until late into the night with their mothers, sisters, and brothers finishing dresses and coats, or making buttons, straw hats, artificial flowers, umbrellas, parasols, and cigars. A manufacturer gave the family the raw materials and paid them

according to how many pieces of work they finished.

If they could, city boys and girls escaped from the boredom of piecework to the excitement and freedom of the city streets. There they found other ways to help their families. They shined shoes and sold gum, peanuts, or anything else that people would buy. The most popular street trade was selling newspapers. By the 1890s, many newspapers were published in the afternoon, which allowed the boys and girls who sold them both to go to school and to work part-time. "Newsies" and other street peddlers were not paid a salary. They were "independent" merchants who bought the newspapers, or whatever else they wanted to sell, for a certain price and then sold them for a slightly higher price on the street. Harry Golden, who sold newspapers to men going home from their work in sweatshops on New York's Lower East Side in the early years of the twentieth century, bought his newspapers for a penny a piece and sold them for two cents. He worked from four o'clock every afternoon until six-thirty and sold a hundred newspapers a day, and when there was a sensational headline, one hundred and fifty.

Working as a newsie was no simple business. Newsies had to be careful that they didn't buy more newspapers than they could sell each day or they would lose money. If they bought too few, they might lose customers. The children also had to remember to keep enough money out of their profits each day to buy their next day's papers. They had to find a good sales spot where there were plenty of people passing by, and they had to attract attention by yelling the headlines when there was

FIGURE 4.8 *These boys and girls who were photographed around 1890 were helping their family by making artificial flowers. If they worked steadily from early morning until late in the evening, they could make about one dollar and twenty cents a day.*

(Jesse Tarbox Beals, "Family Making Artificial Flowers," 1910, Museum of the City of New York, Jacob A. Riis Collection)

FIGURE 4.7 *The foreman of the coal breakers watched for breaker boys who talked, worked too slowly, daydreamed or let slate come down. If he saw one, he would rap him on the back or the head with his stick.*

("Breaker Boys on Shoot," from the collections of the Luzerne County Historical Society)

sensational news. When there was no special news, they sang or danced to make people stop and buy. Buying more newspapers than they could sell, having someone take away their favorite selling spot, or even just a rainy day could ruin a newsie financially.

Another popular activity among city children was "junking." Squads of boys and girls scavenged for fuel, haunting railway yards for bits of coal or picking through vacant lots for wood. According to one former Chicago junker, no one in his neighborhood ever had to buy any fuel, oil, or wood; they collected what their families needed from the railroad tracks. Some children rummaged through trash heaps and dumps looking for newspapers, bottles, rags, and whatever else they could sell to junkyards.

Sometimes junking became stealing. One group of children in Detroit took nine tons of coal, twenty-four baskets of oats, ten barrels of flour, six barrels of sugar, and thirty cases of bottled beer from the railway yards before the police caught up with them. The littlest ones squeezed through pried-open boxcars, while their older brothers and sisters kept watch and carried away the goods.

WORKING AND THE LAW

Almost all Americans believed that it was good for children to work on the family farm with their parents. But as early as the 1830s, a number of community leaders and working men were expressing doubts about how good it was for children to be working in factories and mines. They complained that the long hours children worked in factories kept them from getting even a basic education that would allow them to read the Bible or participate fully in society. Working men also resented the competition

Sweatshops

Many immigrants to New York's Lower East Side at the turn of the twentieth century worked in sweatshops. Sweatshops were factories where clothing was manufactured on an assembly line. A worker would cut out pieces of a garment, then pass the pieces to another worker. As soon as the worker finished his or her part of the job, he or she passed it on to the next worker. A boss walked around the shop, watching and demanding that the workers go faster. The factories were called sweatshops because the employees worked long hours for low wages in miserable, dangerous working conditions.

FIGURE 4.9 *Although more boys sold newspapers than girls, there were a number of girls who worked as "newsies" on the streets of big cities. Many adults feared that working on the streets would harm young girls who later would have to content themselves with spending their days inside the house. These children were photographed with their newspapers in Hartford, Connecticut in March of 1909.*
(Lewis Hine Collection, National Child Labor Committee, Library of Congress)

FIGURE 4.10 *These boys are hauling home firewood they found after an afternoon of scavenging. No one on the street seems to be paying any attention to the boys even though they probably stole the wood from the railroad tracks or from a construction site.*

(Lewis Hine Collection, National Child Labor Committee, Library of Congress)

from children, who worked for less money.

As a result of these concerns, several states eventually passed laws limiting children's work to ten hours a day in manufacturing and mechanical trades. Laws were also passed setting a minimum age at which a child could begin to work in a mill or factory. In the mid-nineteenth century, the minimum age in Connecticut was nine years old. In Massachusetts, children under the age of fifteen were required to attend school for at least three months a year, and they could not work in manufacturing until they were twelve years old.

By the time the Civil War began in 1861, many more children were going to school for at least two or three years before they began working. But there were many parents who still thought work was better training for life than school was. And a large number of families were too poor to be able to forgo their children's labor for long.

In 1870 — the first time the United States census counted the number of working children — one out of every eight children between the ages of ten and fifteen was working. The census did not count the hundreds of thousands of children who worked on farms and in family-owned businesses, did

piecework at home or in sweatshops, worked on the streets, or were hired as maids and nannies. By 1900, the number of children who were working had increased to one out of every six.

In 1904, a group of social workers, church and labor leaders, bankers, educators, and government officials formed the National Child Labor Committee to campaign for federal laws to regulate children's work. Several states already had laws limiting the number of hours children worked in mills, factories, or mines, but nowhere were these laws effectively enforced.

The National Child Labor Committee's campaign for federal laws to regulate the labor of children was opposed by many people who argued that laws limiting children's work would deprive parents of their right to their children's economic help and deny children the right to earn money. Many Americans believed that it was up to parents to decide whether their children worked, not the government.

Finally, when the country was suffering from the biggest economic depression in its history and adults were competing for even the lowest-paying jobs, Congress passed the Fair Labor Standards Act. This act, signed into law by President Franklin Delano Roosevelt in 1938, set standards for minimum

FIGURE 4.11 *This twelve-year-old boy swore that he was sixteen years old so that he could work in this sweatshop pulling the basting threads. To get around the laws setting minimum ages at which children could work, parents lied about how old their children were. The foremen who were hiring underaged children did not object because they could pay them less money than they paid adults.*

(Museum of the City of New York, Jacob A. Riis Collection)

wages and maximum work hours for all workers, including children. With few changes, the Fair Labor Standards Act is still the law today. Federal laws prohibit children under the age of sixteen from working during school hours and limit the number of hours they can work after school and on weekends.

While the campaign to pass laws to regulate children's work was being fought in newspapers and in the halls of government, the number of children working in manufacturing and mining was already dropping on its own. Children were still working in other places, however, and they are still working today. Thousands work in agriculture, where they harvest fruits, vegetables, cotton, and tobacco. Others work in their parents' small businesses. Many more work in stores and as dishwashers, busboys, or waiters in restaurants. Compared to working children a hundred years ago, though, not many children in America today contribute their earnings to their families' upkeep. With few exceptions, they work because they want their own money to spend.

At School

READING, WRITING, ARITHMETIC, RACISM

Salvador Guerrero (b. 1919)

Salvador Guerrero was terrified of his high school English teacher. Mr. Savage was a large, overbearing man with an ugly scar down one cheek who gave his class quizzes every day — and Salvador was failing them all. They were reading Charles Dickens's *A Tale of Two Cities*, and Salvador could not make heads or tails of the story. Spanish was Salvador's native language, and it took him time to understand what he read in English.

When he learned that the movie version of *A Tale of Two Cities* was playing at the St. Angelus theater, Salvador thought that if he could see the movie, his troubles would be over. There was a problem, though. Salvador was a Mexican living in San Angelo, Texas, in the 1930s. At that time, Mexicans were only allowed in the Royal Theater. Salvador went to the St. Angelus theater, hoping against hope that he would be let in. He saw several of his Anglo classmates enter the theater. After working up his courage, he finally approached the ticket counter.

"We can't let you in here," the woman in the box office told him. "We don't have a balcony. You have to go to the Royal."

While Salvador was trying to find the words in English to answer her, a giant of a man came up from behind the ticket counter. "Barbara, are you having any trouble?" he asked. Still trying to translate his feelings of anger, hatred, and humiliation into English words, Salvador realized that it didn't matter what he said. They were not going to let him in.

As he walked away from the ticket counter, the words from Shakespeare's play *As You Like It*, which he had memorized in school, popped into his head.

Sweet are the uses of adversity,
Which, like the toad, ugly and venomous,
Wears yet a precious jewel in his head;
And this our life, exempt from public haunt,
Finds tongues in trees, books in the running brooks,
Sermons in stones, and good in everything.

Remembering the passage made him feel better, though he could not say why those words came to him then.

It is a wonder that Salvador had ever learned those words — or that he went to high school at all. He did not start school until he was nine years old, and then he went for only a few months of the year because his family worked as migrant laborers who followed the harvest.

Every July, with their truck loaded so heavily that it was a miracle it could move, the Guerrero family set off to find work in the fields. For the next several months, they lived in whatever housing the farmers provided. Sometimes it was only a tent in a field. There were no tables, chairs, or toilet facilities other than the fields they worked in. They would come back to San Angelo around Christmastime. That was when Salvador could go to school.

> Salvador did not start school until he was nine years old, and then he went only a few months of the year because his family worked as migrant laborers.

In the late 1920s, when Salvador started school, Mexican children in San Angelo went to the "Mexican school," black children to the "colored school," and white children to "Anglo schools." Until 1926, the education of Mexican children ended in seventh grade.

The school for Mexican children was on the opposite side of town from Salvador's home. There were so many children that they had to go to school in shifts. Salvador attended the afternoon shift. To get to school, he had to walk thirty-five blocks from one end of town to the other in the noonday sun. There was no playground equipment at the school, and even when a boy or girl brought a ball to school, there was no room to play because the yard was too small. Out of sheer boredom, the boys would call each other names and get into fistfights.

Most of the kids that Salvador knew dropped out of school in fourth or fifth grade, as soon as they were old enough to do small jobs around town. The few Mexicans like Salvador who stayed in school were now allowed to transfer to the junior high school, but not until eighth grade; Anglo children went to junior high in the sixth grade. In junior high school, Mexican students were looked down upon by Anglo students, who referred to them as "Meskins." The Mexican boys and girls who had already dropped out of school accused them of trying to act like Anglos.

Salvador Guerrero in 1930 at the age of 11

(Salvador Guerrero)

High school was torture for Salvador. He was not popular, and his academic work was poor. Although he was good at sand-lot football, he was too small to be eligible for the high school football team. He was too shy to ask the few Mexican girls who went to high school for dates. (And Mexican boys like Salvador would not dare ask out an Anglo girl.)

In class, he had trouble keeping up with his assignments. He read slowly because he was always translating the material from English into Spanish in his head. In spite of these difficulties, he stayed in school. To avoid taking chemistry or physics, which he was sure he would fail, he took a public-speaking class, though the very thought of talking in front of class terrified him. To his great surprise, he was good at it.

When Salvador Guerrero graduated from high school, he was encouraged by his speech teacher to apply for a scholarship. He won the scholarship and went to San Angelo Junior College. He was drafted into the United States Army and became a citizen of the United States in 1943. After the war, he moved to Odessa, Texas, where his ability to speak in public became the stepping stone to a career on the radio. Eventually this once-shy boy, who struggled so much in school, was elected county commissioner.

Adapted from Salvador Guerrero, Memorias: A West Texas Life.

At School

Nowadays, almost everyone goes to school five days a week, nine months a year, for at least twelve years. If your parents were born in the United States, most likely they graduated from high school. The same is probably true for your grandparents. Chances are, though, that your great-grandparents did not graduate from high school. And your great-great-grandparents may not have even finished grade school.

Before the 1930s, schooling was a haphazard affair for many white children and most minority children like Salvador Guerrero. How long children stayed in school and the kind of education they received there depended on when they lived and where, whether they were girls or boys, the language their families spoke, and the level of their parents' income. Like today, children whose parents were well off were more likely to stay in school longer and to get a better education than children from poor families. What has changed is that today more children than ever before spend the years between six and sixteen as students in free, tax-supported public schools.

NOT REQUIRED

Until 1836, there were no laws anywhere in the United States that children had to go to school. In that year, Massachusetts passed a law insisting that children under the age of fifteen who worked in manufacturing had to attend school for three out of every twelve months. But in many areas of the country, especially in rural areas of the South, there were no schools for children to go to. Children who didn't live far from a school dropped in for a few months of the year and then dropped out to work. Usually they left school altogether after only a few years. President Abraham Lincoln was never able to go to any school regularly. By some estimates, his total time in school was less than a year of his life.

COUNTRY SCHOOLS

In most country schools, up to sixty children, ranging in age from four or five to eighteen or even twenty, were crammed together in one classroom. It was not unusual for children to share a desk with a seatmate. Hamlin Garland and his seatmate Burton Babcock became close friends. But not all seatmates became friends. Lucy Larcom's seatmate at her new school offered to do her sums for her when she saw that Lucy could not do them. Lucy accepted her offer, but afterward she felt like a "miserable cheat" and did not like the girl who she thought looked down on her.

FIGURE 5.1 *The interior of a country school in Iowa in 1893. Depending on how close a child sat to the stove in winter, the room was either blazing hot or freezing cold. In summer, with no air conditioning, everyone sweltered in the heat which made them drowsy and irritable. Many country schools also had no toilet facilities and the children had to relieve themselves in the woods. Few had playgrounds or playground equipment.*

("Bear Creek Township School," 1893, State Historical Society of Iowa, Des Moines)

The teacher's desk was in the corner or the front of the room facing the children. In the middle of the room was a big iron stove that constantly had to be fed firewood. Hamlin Garland recalled that in his prairie school, it was "always too hot or too cold . . . and on certain days, when a savage wind beat and clamored at the loose windows, the girls, humped and shivering, sat upon their feet to keep them warm, and the younger children with shawls over their shoulders sought permission to gather close about the stove."

Since most Americans lived on farms and in small towns that served farming communities, the school year was tied to the agricultural work cycle. There were two terms — the winter term (which began after Thanksgiving when the harvest was finished) and the summer term (which began after the spring planting in May). Older boys, whose labor was needed on the farm at other times of the year, went to school in the winter term. They were usually taught by men because school boards believed that boys needed a strong hand to control them. Girls attended the summer term, which was when women were allowed to teach. Only later were women permitted to teach both terms.

EDUCATING GIRLS

Until the late eighteenth century (and even after that), it was widely believed that educating girls was a waste of time and money because they were all going to become wives and mothers. Public opinion began to change around the time of the American Revolution as some men realized that mothers had an important influence on society. Women needed to be educated, these men argued, so that they could mold the minds of their children. As a result of this change in attitude, girls were permitted to attend school during the winter term along with the boys.

TEACHERS AND HOW THEY TAUGHT

The main requirement for teaching school was to be able to keep order in the classroom. Most teachers kept order by brute force. Lucy Larcom recalled in her memoir that when she moved to Lowell, Massachusetts, in 1835, she was terrified of her teacher — a tall, gaunt man who stalked across the classroom, right over

the desktops, if he suspected that there was any mischief going on. She had seen him punish the children, even the little girls, by hitting them on the palm of their hands with a thick leather strap. And once he punished a boy, whom he had caught annoying his seatmate, by chasing him around the schoolroom and sticking a pin into his shoulder whenever he caught up with him.

Women teachers, who were not as physically strong, were more likely than male teachers to rely on shaming their students by isolating them or making them wear dunce caps when they misbehaved or failed their lessons. They also were more likely to gain their students' cooperation by rewarding them with privileges and prizes than by punishing them.

Some teachers failed to keep order. In the five years

Corporal PUNISHMENT

A new teacher in a school in Hamilton, Ohio, in the 1840s tried to take a different approach to discipline in his classroom. He told the children that he hoped never to have to use the rods he found lying on his desk. He broke the sticks and burned them in the stove and called the children to order. But the children, who were used to being ruled by fear, did not come to order then or later. They whispered and giggled and began scuffling and pushing one another. The boys passed notes to the girls. They held up their slates with messages written on them that would make the girls laugh. They threw spitballs at one another. Finally, things became so bad that the teacher had to use force, but the big boys would not stand for it. They fought the teacher and hit him back when he whipped them.

Adapted from W.D. Howells'
A Boy's Town

between 1832 and 1837, more than three hundred Massachusetts schools were closed for periods of time because the teachers could not control the children. In some towns, teachers were routinely turned out of their schools by the students. In New Hampshire at the beginning of the nineteenth century, for example, the older boys would select a day to stay behind when the smaller children left at lunchtime. When the teacher, who was a stranger to the area and did not know the custom, went to eat his lunch, the boys barricaded the doors and windows so that he could not get back into the school. Then they spent the rest of the afternoon having fun.

Teachers tended to be young. They had no formal training and sometimes knew little more than the children they were teaching. Daniel Drake suspected all along that one of his teachers did not know much. His suspicion was confirmed when he came to the "Double Rule of Three" in his mathematics book, for his teacher was no better than he was at finding the sum. Many teachers were only able to spell a little, do some arithmetic, and read without stumbling over the big words. They taught by making their students memorize the material they were expected to learn and then asking them to recite it back to them. There were few explanations and no discussions.

WHAT THEY WERE TAUGHT

At the beginning of the term, the teacher would group different children together based on their ability, not their age. The beginners started with a primer that taught them the ABC's and to read simple sentences like "Rab sees the frog. Can the frog see Rab?" When they finished with the primer, they moved on to the first reader, the second reader, and so on. By the time they reached the fifth reader, they were able to read and memorize passages like this one from "The Village Blacksmith," by Henry Wadsworth Longfellow:

FIGURE 5.2 *In this schoolhouse, the schoolmaster is dictating spelling words to his students who are "toeing the line." To be at the head of the line was to be ranked first, while to be at the foot of the line was to be last.*

(L. Taylor, "The District School," 1900, Library of Congress)

Under a spreading chestnut tree
The village smithy stands;
The smith, a mighty man is he,
With large and sinewy hands;
And the muscles of his brawny arms
Are strong as iron bands.

The children moved through the books at their own pace. If the lesson in the second reader was too hard for them, they went back to the first reader.

In arithmetic, most children did not go beyond learning to add, subtract, multiply, divide whole numbers, and calculate fractions in arithmetic. A few advanced students learned to do word problems that required them to understand ratios and proportions. They also learned some basic geography, history, and grammar.

Several times a day, the children were called up in small groups to the front of the room to recite their lessons for the teacher. Sometimes the younger students not only learned their own lessons, but by hearing the older children, they learned theirs, too. But some children were so terrified of making a mistake when they were called up that everything would become blurry and their tongues would be unable to form the words. Disgraced in front of all the other children, they would slink back to their place on the bench.

Recess and lunchtime were favorite times of day. Children brought their lunches from home and ate them sitting on the benches in winter, and on a log in the schoolyard at other times of the year. Instead of peanut butter and jelly sandwiches or pizza for lunch, children brought such things as bread and butter, bread and jam, pies with meat in them, or bits of meat wrapped up in a piece of paper. Hamlin Garland recalled that in winter, their dinner pails, which were stored in the entryway to the school, were often frozen solid and they had to thaw out their minced pie or bread and butter by putting it on the stove.

Once they were done eating at Daniel Drake's country school, the children swung on grapevines, hunted for nuts, and climbed trees in search of birds' nests and persimmons and other fruits. They also shot arrows, played ball, ran races, and played a game called prisoner's base. At Maria Foster's small-town school, the girls used to play under the apple tree, while the boys played out in the street. This informal separation, with boys playing their games in one place and girls playing their games in another, was not unusual and still occurs to some extent today.

MOVING INTO THE MODERN ERA

In the second half of the nineteenth century, as attendance increased, schools in the more settled parts of the country and in big cities began to resemble the public schools we have today. State after state passed laws that made public schools tax-supported, locally controlled institutions that were free to all children. There was a shift to age-graded classrooms in towns and cities where there were enough children the same age. Report cards began to be used. And increasingly, teachers attended a summer institute or a few years of normal school (the equivalent of the first two years of high school), where they were given some training before they started to teach.

Following Massachusetts's lead, several states passed laws making schooling compulsory for at least a few months a year for children under a certain age. By the 1880s, many children were going to school for about five years before dropping out. Some returned later, particularly boys living on the frontier, who bounced back and forth for years between working and going to school. As a result, many did not finish their schooling until they were in their twenties.

In the far West, where families lived miles apart from one

FIGURE 5.3 *A one-room sod school house in Custer County, Nebraska. By 1889, it is likely that the teacher in this picture had some training in teaching even though she did not have a college education. Many of the women who went into teaching were in their late teens or early twenties and taught only for a few years before quitting to get married.*

(Solomon Butcher, "Sod School," District 62, Nebraska Historical Society, Photographic Collection)

another on widely scattered homesteads and ranches, children attended one-room schoolhouses well into the twentieth century (and in some places they still do). In remote areas of states like Arizona and New Mexico, where there were few schools, children were taught at home by their parents or sent away to school. Some ranching families believed that their children's education was so important that they moved to town in the winter so that their children could attend school. Other families boarded their children with teachers, relatives, or friends in town. United States Supreme Court Justice Sandra Day O'Connor, whose family lived on a remote ranch on the New Mexico–Arizona border, was sent to live with her grandmother in Texas when she was just five years old so that she could go to school.

AFRICAN-AMERICAN CHILDREN IN THE NORTH AND SOUTH

In all parts of the country, African-American children have been given an education unequal to the education given white children. Before the Civil War, African-American children were forced to attend separate schools in Massachusetts, New York, Rhode Island, Illinois, Indiana, Ohio, Pennsylvania, California, and several other states. In 1833, Prudence Crandall, a Quaker, was arrested and put in jail when she admitted an African-American girl to her girls' school in Canterbury, Connecticut.

In the North, schools for African-American children were given less money to operate than white schools even though black parents paid the same taxes as white parents. In 1849, parents of children attending the segregated school for black children in Boston petitioned the Boston School Committee to integrate the schools, saying that the separate schools were neglected and inferior to the white schools. The committee

FIGURE 5.4 *In 1848, five-year-old Sarah Roberts was denied the opportunity to attend the primary school nearest her home because she was African American. When her father took the school committee to court in 1849, the courts decided in favor of the school committee. Six years later, the Massachusetts legislature passed a law that made it illegal to segregate school children on the basis of their race, color or religion.*

(Photographs and Prints Division, Schomburg Center for Research in Black Culture, New York Public Library, Astor, Lenox and Tilden Foundations)

FIGURE 5.5 *In the years immediately after the Civil War, schools for blacks were organized all over the South with the help of the Freedman's Bureau. These schools were attended by people of all ages who were eager to learn to read.*

(Photograph and Prints Division, Schomburg Center for Research in Black Culture, New York Public Library, Astor, Lenox and Tilden Foundations)

refused, telling the parents that their children's "peculiar physical, mental, and moral structure, requires an educational treatment, different . . . from that of white children."

The situation for African-American children in the South was even worse than it was in the North. In the South, there were just a few private schools for free African-American children, and there were no schools at all for slaves. In the 1830s, laws were passed in all the Southern states except Kentucky forbidding anyone to teach a slave to read. A common punishment for learning to write was to cut off the forefinger of the slave's right hand.

A few slaves learned to read anyway. One of those who learned was Frederick Douglass, who eventually escaped from slavery to become a famous speaker, newspaper editor, and writer in the antislavery movement. His master, Hugh Auld, exploded in anger when he discovered that his wife, Sophia, was teaching Frederick to read. He told her, "A nigger should know nothing but to obey his master — to do as he is told to do. Learning would spoil the best nigger in the world." After this conversation, if Sophia Auld found Frederick with a book or newspaper, she would rip it out of his hands and scold him.

Sophia Auld's behavior only strengthened Frederick's determination to learn to read. He wrote in his autobiography that he made friends with white boys that he met on the streets of Baltimore and traded them bread for lessons. He carried his book with him whenever he went on an errand and tried to make time for a lesson before he returned home. He learned to write by copying the four letters ("L," "S," "A," "F") that he saw ships' carpenters write on the timbers to indicate the part of the ship for which the board was intended. "[W]hen I met with any boy who I knew could write, I would tell him I could write as well as he. The next word would be, 'I don't believe you. Let me see you try it.' I would then make the letters . . . and ask him to beat that. In this way I got a good many lessons in writing."

In the five years following the Civil War, more than four thousand schools were set up for African Americans in the South. Poor black communities organized school committees, raised the money to buy land, and built schools. They paid the teachers with the assistance of the Freedmen's Bureau, which was set up by the federal government to help emancipated slaves. White Southerners who were opposed to these schools sometimes burned them down and drove the teachers away. Their opposition did not stop former slaves of all ages from flocking to them. So many former slaves were eager to learn that schools had to turn students away.

Paying for PUBLIC SCHOOL

Few public schools were free in the early years of this nation's history. They were supported by a combination of taxes, private donations, and fees paid by the parents of the students.

Laws establishing free public education for all children in the South — white and African American — were passed by black and Republican dominated state legislatures following the Civil War. The schools were segregated by race, with white children attending one set of schools and African-American children attending a separate set of schools. Both white and African-American schools in the South had shorter school terms and were more poorly attended than public schools in other parts of the country. In 1890, for example, only 53 percent of all children — white or black — were enrolled in public schools in the South, as compared to 61 percent in other parts of the country. Many children did not go to school because their parents were

FIGURE 5.6 *A segregated first grade classroom in Gees Bend, Alabama. The pupils are of all ages. The grown man, shown standing near the blackboard is just learning to read.*

(Marion Post Wolcott, 1939, Library of Congress)

too poor to buy them the clothes or shoes they needed.

Among Southern schools, schools for African-American children were the poorest. In 1910, for example, schools for white children in Lowndes County, Alabama, were open seven months a year, while those for African-American children were open only four months. Teachers in white schools were paid as much as four times the amount that teachers in black schools were paid. In the 1896–1897 school year, the state of Maryland spent an average of $8.93 for the education of every white child, while spending only $4.18 for every African-American student.

BEING AMERICANIZED

One of the major missions of the public schools was to turn immigrant and Native American children into "Americans." Americanizing Native American children usually meant taking them away from their parents and sending them to boarding schools far away from their reservations. (Indian reservations are territories that have been set aside for a particular tribe by the federal government.) Indian boarding schools were founded by Christian missionaries with the support of the federal government to speed Indian assimilation into the white world. Many government leaders, missionaries, and other influential white people thought that once Native Americans adopted white ways, they would be less likely to make trouble for European Americans by claiming land that they had once lived on.

Against many parents' objections, Native American children were rounded up by the United States Army, placed in wagons, and taken to these boarding schools under armed guard. Lone Foot, a member of the Blackfoot tribe, recalled, "It was very cold that day when we were loaded into the wagons. None of us wanted to go and our parents didn't want us to go. Oh, we cried for this was the first time we were to be separated from our parents. . . ."

FIGURE 5.7 *These children are going to a segregated school for black children in Gee's Bend, Alabama in 1937. Note the separate entrances for boys and girls.*

(Arthur Rothstein, Library of Congress)

FIGURE 5.8 *Chiricahua Apache youth when they arrived at the Carlisle Indian School in Pennsylvania. The second picture was taken a few months later. Their hair had been cut, their blankets and buckskin clothing had been taken from them, and they were given "white-man's" clothes to wear as part of the school's program.*

(National Anthropological Archives, Smithsonian Institution)

At the Indian boarding schools, the children were punished if they spoke anything but English. They were not fed a healthy diet or given decent health care. The dormitories where the children slept were overcrowded, and diseases spread quickly from one child to another. On Sundays, they were taken to chapel, where they prayed to Jesus. Many Native American children became homesick for their families and ran away. When they were caught by police, they were brought back to school and punished by the school authorities.

Work was considered to be an important part of the training at the Indian boarding schools, just as it was in orphanages and reform schools. The children were required to work, not just to learn but to keep their schools running. The schools did not have enough money to operate without their labor. Girls cooked, sewed, and mended for the students. Boys raised livestock for food and made shoes for other students. They even built and repaired the schools' buildings.

Native American parents complained that Indian boarding schools did not educate their children for life among their own people and that even after they attended these schools they were not accepted by white people. After fifty years, even the federal government had to admit that the Indian boarding schools had failed. During the 1930s, the government began to close them. Native American children were sent to Indian day schools on their reservations or to the public schools near where they lived.

Though the process of Americanizing immigrant children was not as brutal as that faced by Native American children, it was harsh. Public schools were not welcoming places for any child who did not speak English, especially if their families were Catholic or Jewish. In most schools, English was the only language the children were permitted to speak. Immigrant children were often terrified when they were first brought to school and they realized that they did not understand a word of what was being said. Marie Jastrow, who came to New York from Hungary in 1907, recalled, "I had no choice but to learn the new language, quickly and without fuss. Not much help was offered. Few teachers were linguists and the feelings of the greenhorns in the class were not spared."

According to Harry Golden, the first words immigrant boys learned when they went to school on New York's Lower East Side were swearwords. The kids would instruct the newcomer, "When the teacher says, 'Good morning,' you say . . ." and they would teach him a swearword. Then, when the boy did as he was told, the entire

Going to an
INDIAN SCHOOL

In 1883, Sun Elk was the first Hopi boy from the Taos pueblo in New Mexico to attend the Carlisle Indian School. He recalled his experience there: "[A] white man — what you call an Indian Agent — came and took all of us who were in that school far off on a train to a new kind of village called Carlisle Indian School, and I stayed there seven years. . . .

"They told us that Indian ways were bad. They said we must get civilized. I remember that word too. It means 'be like the white man.' I am willing to be like the white man, but I did not believe that Indian ways were wrong. But they kept teaching us for seven years. And the books told how bad the Indians had been to the white men — burning their towns and killing their women and children. But I had seen white men do that to Indians. We all wore white man's clothes and ate white man's food and went to white man's churches and spoke white man's talk. And so after a while we also began to say Indians were bad. We laughed at our own people and their blankets and cooking pots and sacred societies and dances. I tried to learn the lessons — and after seven years I came home."

Adapted from Sun Elk, "He is not one of us."
In Native American Testimony

class would laugh at him. Harry fell for this trick on his second day of school and couldn't wait for his chance to pull it on the next newcomer.

In some schools, immigrant children were given a few weeks of intensive English lessons before being sent to a regular classroom. Older children who did not speak English were put back into first grade, where they had to sit with little children at desks that were too small for them. Many immigrant children responded by leaving school as soon as possible.

Learning to speak English was only the first step in becoming "Americanized." On the playground, immigrant children were told to forget the games they had played in their native

FIGURE 5.9 *These immigrant children were being given a lesson in American patriotism at their New York City school, where they were taught to salute the flag and to sing "My Country 'Tis of Thee."*

(Museum of the City of New York, Jacob A. Riis Collection)

countries and to play baseball, kickball, and basketball. In home economics classes, girls were taught to prepare American foods, which sometimes included foods that children were forbidden to eat by their religion, such as pork. They were also forced to recite "The Lord's Prayer," even if they were Jewish.

BEYOND GRAMMAR SCHOOL

In the late eighteenth and early nineteenth centuries, any boy or girl who wanted an education beyond the one offered by the grammar school had to go to a private academy, a boarding school, or the preparatory department of colleges like Harvard and Yale. Boys' academies had classes in Latin and Greek, which were required for admission to college, as well as algebra, geometry, and chemistry. Private academies for girls offered classes in fine needlework, dancing, painting, and music in addition to the standard classes in reading, arithmetic, writing, history, and geography. As people's views about educating girls changed, private schools for girls began offering classes in subjects like Latin, Greek, and chemistry that previously had been available only to boys.

The first public high school was created in Boston in 1821 to educate boys who wanted to pursue a career in business or law. It had a three-year course of studies that included arithmetic, geography, history, English, bookkeeping, and science. Not many boys enrolled, and most of those who did dropped out and went to work before they graduated. The first public high school for girls opened its doors in Boston in 1825. By contrast, it was enormously popular. The students were motivated, their attendance was good, and they did better than the boys on the citywide high school exam, even though there was only one teacher for 133 girls.

Boston mayor Josiah Quincy was alarmed by the success of the girls' school. He did not believe that girls needed a high school education. After all, he argued, they were only going to be homemakers and mothers. He convinced the Boston School Committee that providing a high school education for every girl who wanted one would drain the city's treasury. Despite its success, the girls' high school was closed after only a year. This setback did not dampen the determination of girls to get a high school education. Parents continued to pressure school boards in cities where there were high schools for boys to establish high schools for girls.

GOING TO HIGH SCHOOL

After the Civil War, a growing number of children began to stay in school long enough to go to high school. Most high schools were coeducational because it was too expensive to maintain separate schools for boys and girls. Those opposed to educating boys and girls together argued that because boys and girls are different biologically, they need to be taught differently. One critic of coeducation even went so far as to argue that overloading girls' brains in high school would interfere with their ability to have children later on.

Neither girls nor their parents seem to have paid much attention to these warnings. Girls continued to enroll in coeducational high schools, where they took classes with boys in physics, chemistry, physiology, geography, algebra, geometry, Latin, Greek, German, history, rhetoric, and English literature. Like boys, they enrolled in the business and commercial courses when they were available.

Teenage girls often had better grades than boys in high school. They also graduated from high school at a higher rate than boys. One reason that girls stayed in high school was that they had fewer choices available to them than boys did. Teaching was one of the few respectable kinds of paid work that were open to middle-class girls, and it required a high school education. Many middle-class parents considered high school a safe place for their daughters to be until they were old enough to marry.

Americanizing NAMES

*T*eachers often gave immigrant children new, more American names without consulting them or their parents. When Leonard Covello's father saw his son's report card and noticed that the teacher had changed the spelling of the family's name, he asked his son, "What is this? 'Leonard Covello'! What happened to the 'i' in 'Coviello'? . . . From 'Leonardo' to 'Leonard' I can follow. . . . But you don't change a family name. A name is a name. What happened to the 'i'?"

Leonard explained that his teacher found "Covello" easier to say and that he wanted it that way, too. His father thumped him on the head. "What has this Mrs. Cutter got to do with my name?"

"It's more American. The 'i' doesn't help anything," Leonard tried to explain.

His mother took his father's side in the argument. "A person's life and his honor is in his name. He never changes it. A name is not a shirt or a piece of underwear."

Leonard told her that she didn't understand.

"What is there to understand? Now that you have become Americanized, you understand everything and I understand nothing."

Adapted from Leonard Covello and Guido D'Agostino, The Heart Is the Teacher.

Teenage boys had more options. If they wanted more training, they could go to private business schools and attend short courses in the subjects they needed. They could attend the preparatory departments of colleges. They could begin to learn a skilled trade on the job. And if they wanted to work, there was a wide variety of jobs that did not require them to have a high school diploma. With all these alternatives, boys were less likely to stay in high school until they graduated.

By 1900, more children were going to school than ever before — roughly 72 percent of the children between the ages of five and seventeen were enrolled. Most children did not stay long enough to earn a high school diploma. But over the next forty years, this situation changed drastically. Kate Simon recalled that when she graduated from elementary school (which had eight grades) in the mid 1920s, her father said that if she insisted on going to high school, it would be only for a year — "a year in which I would study typing and stenography to prepare me for a job. . . ." As the end of the school year approached and her father kept reminding her that she was going to have to find a job soon, Kate was at a loss for what to do. How was she going to find a job at the age of fourteen with no skill? She was rescued by the principal of her school, who wrote her father a letter saying that "a girl of my interests and capa-

FIGURE 5.10 *Girls and boys are sitting in separate rows in this high school biology class. Many adults thought it a bad idea to mix the sexes in high school.*

(Frances Benjamin Johnston, 1899, Library of Congress)

bilities should be offered the broader education of a general high school. . . ." Her father bowed to the authority of the principal and Kate continued her education.

By 1940, 95 percent of all children in America between the ages of five and seventeen were in school, and nearly half of them were staying in school through twelfth grade. Today, more than sixty years later, nearly 90 percent of all children graduate from high school, and a considerable number go on to college.

At Play *and in* Love

FUN, FRIENDS, AND FREEDOM

William Dean Howells (1837–1920)

It may be hard to believe that children managed to have any fun in the days before mass-produced toys, computers, video games, television, and movies. But people who grew up in those days will tell you that they had fun without those devices. Lots of it.

William Dean Howells wrote fondly about those long ago days. He was a boy in the 1840s in Hamilton, Ohio, where children could run around the street or town at any time of day without their parents worrying about their safety. The main attraction for boys in Hamilton was the Miami River and the canal basin, especially in the summer. They loved the thrill of diving into deep swimming holes and the fun of splashing around in the shallower areas of the river. Colored clays from the riverbank turned into war paint during their "Indian fights." Sometimes the boys would even venture over to the island in the center of the river. That meant gathering their clothes into a bundle that they would hold on their heads with one hand while swimming across with the other. On the island, they would lay out under the trees, telling each other stories.

Like children today, William and his friends loved outdoor adventures and games. And like parents today, the mothers of Hamilton had strict rules. William remembers how many of his friends' mothers forbade their sons to go in the river. Sometimes those who disobeyed gave themselves away by coming home with water still dripping from their hair and their shirts inside out. Sometimes they even came home shirtless — the boys would trick one another by tying shirtsleeves in knots and wetting them so they were impossible to untie.

Staying cooped up indoors in winter was as tiresome for William and his friends as it is for modern children. As soon as the water in the canal froze, the boys in Hamilton took out their ice skates and started racing each other. In those days, boys and girls did not go to a store and buy ready-made ice skates. They bought blades attached to pieces of wood, which they took to a carpenter, who made holes for straps by piercing the wood. Then, if they could afford it, they went to a saddle maker, who made straps for them. If leather straps were too expensive, they tied their skates on with strings. Even though the skates were always coming off, they still had a good time flying around the ice, playing tag, and trying out different figures.

Just when the children had their fill of winter, spring came and they could play ball again. Their favorite ball game was called three-cornered cat, a game very much like baseball. As the weather grew warmer, William's friends took off their shoes and started running races. They climbed trees. They played hide-and-seek in the neighborhood sheds and barns and tag in empty lots.

William's friends were fiercely competitive at their

William Dean Howells

(Houghton Library, Harvard University)

games. Kite flying in the commons was popular, and the boys spent lots of time talking about the design of their kites and tinkering with them so that they would stay up in the air longer and fly higher than anyone else's. They played marbles for keeps, taking all the marbles they won. With so much at stake, the boys were always quarreling about whether a marble was in or out of the ring, the same way boys and girls argue about the referee's calls in a soccer game today.

Some of William's friends could launch and control tops as well as a good baseball pitcher controls his pitches. A skilled player was admired by all the boys. Their tops were made on a lathe owned by the father of one of William's friends. A boy would launch his top into a ring, and the other boys would wait until the top began to settle in and spin silently. Then any other boy had a right to aim his top at it, and if he hit it, he won the first boy's top.

Few of William's friends owned guns, but they all dreamed of having one. Several of them would go hunting, sharing one of their fathers' shotguns, and take turns beating the bushes for birds, shooting, and retrieving. But hunting was more than just shooting; it was a ritual of getting up at four in the morning, when everything that was familiar by day became strange in the pale light of morning. William enjoyed the mounting tension as they waited in the morning stillness, which was broken by the whirring of wings as the ducks arrived and the shooting began.

Having a gun was also handy for making noise during celebrations. On Christmas Eve, before the church bells began to ring, the boys in Hamilton shot off their guns. They also lit firecrackers and small torpedoes. They made as much noise as possible on the Fourth of July. And Easter wasn't just a solemn holiday; it was also the occasion for Easter egg fights. Right after breakfast on Easter Sunday, everyone would run out of the house with colored eggs and begin to fight with them by striking the little ends of the eggs together. The boy or girl whose egg didn't break had the right to take the other kid's egg.

The fun and freedom of running around Hamilton with his friends came to an end when William Dean Howells was eleven years old and his family moved. By then, he was already setting type in his father's print shop. Soon after, he began spending most of his time in the shop, helping to publish his father's newspaper and delivering it to the subscribers. As an adult, William Dean Howells was the editor of two of the most influential magazines of his day.

Adapted from William Dean Howells, A Boy's Town.

> In those days, boys and girls did not go to a store and buy ready-made ice skates. They bought blades attached to pieces of wood.

At Play and in Love

If a time machine sent you back to the 1840s when William Dean Howells was growing up, you would have no trouble recognizing many of the things he and his friends did for fun. But if a boy or girl from the 1840s were suddenly put down in the middle of an American city today, they would be astonished by many of the things children do for fun, like going to the movies or going shopping, exploring the Internet, and playing computer games. They would also be surprised to see how many new toys there are, and how some of the old ones have changed. But what might surprise them most is the amount of free time modern kids have. In William Dean Howells's day, many boys and girls were working more than ten hours a day by the time they were thirteen or fourteen years old.

TIME TO PLAY

The need to work did not mean that children could never play. It only meant that they didn't have as much time to play. Most boys and girls managed to enjoy themselves whenever they had a chance. At lunchtime, boys and girls who worked in factories, mills, and mines played ball games, keep-away, marbles, and mumblety-peg; they read books and gossiped with each other. Even when they were supposed to be working, they found ways to play. They rode the shafting belts on the cotton looms up to the ceiling or made balls out of odds and ends of string so they could play catch. Lucy Larcom, who went to work in a cotton mill when she was eleven, recalled, "We were not occupied more than half the time. The intervals [between work] were spent frolicking around the spinning-frames, teasing and talking to the older girls, or entertaining ourselves with games and stories in a corner, or exploring, with the overseer's permission, the mysteries of the carding-room, the dressing room, and the weaving room."

Boys working in the breakers in the coal-mining industry threw grease balls dunked in coal dust from the top of the breakers onto unsuspecting boys below them and hazed newcomers by wrestling them to the ground, pulling their pants off, and rubbing axle grease all over them. Using finger spelling, they communicated with each other when the breaker boss's back was turned.

Sometimes work was turned into a social community event. In rural areas, people came together to build houses, stables, and barns or to roll logs, husk corn, and sew quilts. "Harvest was a kind of frolic," Daniel Drake recalled. "When the crop was drawn in, the ears were heaped into a long pile or rick, a night fixed on, and the neighbors notified. . . . As they assembled at nightfall the green glass quart whisky-bottle . . . was handed to every one, man and boy, as they arrived to take a drink." When enough people had arrived, the men and boys

FIGURE 6.1 *For many boys, splashing and diving and sunning themselves along a river bank was the essence of summer fun.*

(*Chicago Daily News,* 1919, Chicago Historical Society)

divided into teams and there was a contest to see which team could finish husking its pile of corn first. It was a fierce contest, with cheating, lying, and fights. At the end, the captain of the victorious team was carried in triumph on the shoulders of one of his teammates amid shouts of victory.

MAKING YOUR OWN FUN

A lot of the things that children do for fun today depend on using manufactured toys and equipment like baseball gloves, footballs, tennis rackets, Barbie dolls, PlayStations, and skateboards. Two hundred years ago, few of these toys existed. Like everything else families used, toys were usually homemade. Balls were made from pig bladders or from string and rags. Dolls were made from scraps of fabric and yarn. Seashells, gourds, and leaves served as toy dishes. Sleds were put together from pieces of wood. Many boys made their own tops and kites in the way William Dean Howells and his friends did. They even made their own marbles out of clay.

With few toys and no commercial entertainment like movies or television to amuse them, children made their own fun. Like you, they went swimming and boating and played on the beach in summer. In winter, they went sledding and ice-skating and had snowball fights. Building forts, hideouts, and tree houses kept them busy for days on end. Outdoors, they played tag, hide-and-seek, and other games that are still enjoyed today. Indoors, they played with their pets, joked around with their friends and brothers and sisters, and played board games like lotto, checkers, and chess.

Playing ball was as popular with boys in 1840 as it is today. But in those days, ball games were usually informal affairs among children who went to the same school or who lived in the same neighborhood. Adult-run organizations with teams and competitions, like Pop Warner Football or Little League Baseball, did not get their start until the twentieth century.

In the days before movies and television, books were the inspiration for a lot of make-believe play. William Dean Howells loved a story called "The Greek Soldier," which was about a young Greek man who fought against the Turks for his country's independence. In their fantasy games, William was always the Greek soldier who led the other boys into battle against the Turks.

PLAYING WITH THE GIRLS

Girls played with their brothers and sometimes played with other

FIGURE 6.2 *Marbles was a popular game with boys throughout the eighteenth and nineteenth centuries. The point of the game was to shoot your opponent's marbles out of the ring in which they were placed. Older boys sometimes bet on marble games even though grown-ups disapproved.*

(Bain Collection, Library of Congress)

FIGURE 6.3 *Most girls played with homemade rag dolls like the one pictured here. We do not know if this doll belonged to an African American child or to a white child. But by the looks of her, she was not left to lie in the toy box untouched.*

(Courtesy "The Quaker Collection," Atwater Kent Museum)

boys as well, but often they preferred to play with other girls. When they were young, girls enjoyed playing house, playing school, and having pretend tea parties, weddings, and funerals. Jumping rope and seeing how fast and long a girl could jump before she tripped was a favorite challenge, and so was a good game of pick-up sticks or jacks. Before the 1870s, store-bought dolls were usually expensive. Before the invention of plastic, their heads, which were usually made of china, were easily broken. In many families they were more showpieces to be taken out and admired than something a child could play with. Dorothy Howard, who lived in Texas at the beginning of the twentieth century, reported that the china dolls were never the "babies" in the games of house when she was young. That role was reserved for the rag dolls her grandmother made for her. They had black shoe-button eyes and a nose and mouth drawn with ink and they came with their own wardrobes, complete with lace-edged underskirts.

GETTING TOGETHER AND COURTING

As they grew older, boys and girls lost interest in many of the activities that they thought were fun when they were younger. Like modern teenagers, they began to look for ways to become acquainted and have fun with members of the opposite sex. While boys and girls are still likely to meet in the same way and in many of the same places that they met one another 150 years ago, the processes of getting to know one another and courting have changed.

During the eighteenth and nineteenth centuries, the rituals of courtship were more tightly controlled by parents than they are today. These rituals differed for middle-class and working-class teens. When a middle-class young man liked a young woman, he asked her if he might call on her. If she said yes, the

FIGURE 6.4 *Like today, one of the main places that boys and girls met and started to pair off was in school. This engraving shows a group of boys competing to walk a popular girl home from school and carry her books.*

(*The Reigning Belle, Harper's Weekly,* July 2, 1877, p.557. Library of Congress)

FIGURE 6.5 *Young people dance to the music of a fiddler. Dancing was a pastime enjoyed by rich and poor alike. The rich took dancing lessons, while the poor were taught by their sisters and brothers and friends, or picked up the dance steps by observing others.*

(William Sidney Mount, *Rustic Dance After a Sleigh Ride*, 1830. Museum of Fine Arts, Boston)

young man came and sat with her in the parlor or on the front porch of her family's home. With her mother, father, brothers, and sisters looking on, the couple tried to get to know each other better. If the young man came often, he was considered to be courting the young woman. It was expected that the young man would eventually ask the young woman to marry him. Though American parents usually did not choose their children's marriage partners for them, most young women wanted their parents' approval before they agreed to marry a young man.

Middle-class parents could afford to be more protective of their daughters than could most working-class families. Parents who were poor usually didn't have the time, the energy,

or the kind of homes where they could keep a careful watch on their daughters. They often lived in cramped, crowded rooms, which made it impossible, or at least uncomfortable, for a boy to come calling. Anne Ellis wrote about the cabin where she lived with her family: "Any one coming to see me had his courage with him, as there was no place to entertain except in the kitchen or front room and Mama's bed was there."

With nowhere else to go, working-class boys and girls met outside their homes. Groups of boys and groups of girls would stroll along city streets, in parks, in fields, on riverbanks, and on beaches, looking for each other.

Everybody had opinions about young men and women who

were romantically linked or who they thought should be. Matchmaking was a primary source of entertainment for many people. As Eliza Southgate Bowne wrote to her cousin in 1802, "The prevailing propensity this winter is match-making, and at the assemblies there is no other conversation, — such and such a one will make a match because they dance together, —

another one is positively engaged because she does not dance with him. If a lady does not attend the assembly constantly — 'tis because her favorite swain is not a member, — if she does — 'tis to meet him there: if she is silent, she is certainly in love; if she is gay and talks much, there must be a lover in the way."

Everyone, rich and poor, believed that it was the girl's duty

♥ · ♥ · ♥ · ♥ · ♥ · ♥ · ♥ · ♥ · ♥ · ♥ · **FIRST** Love · ♥ · ♥ · ♥ · ♥ · ♥ · ♥ · ♥ · ♥ · ♥

Jim Chipman was Anne Ellis's first love. He was not the kind of boy mothers approve of, but Anne didn't care. She was attracted to him from the first time she laid eyes on him at her school in the mining town of Bonanza, Colorado, in the late 1880s. Anne was about ten years old, and Jim was a few years older.

Every evening, Anne wished on the first star she saw that Jim loved her. Whenever she had a chance, she dropped apple peelings over her shoulder, hoping they would land in the shape of a *J* or a *C*. She counted fence posts and flower petals, reciting "He loves me, he loves me not," always trying to pick the right number so that she would end on "He loves me." She went to the store where he worked in the summers, paraded by his house, and even convinced her mother to visit his mother.

For a while, it seemed as if Jim did like her. At Christmastime, he gave her a rose-colored velvet sewing box, and at Easter, he gave her a booklet in the shape of a butterfly with a poem inside. When at school he sang, "My Annie's eyes are

blue, They'll be black 'fore I get through," Anne was so overjoyed that he called her "my Annie" that she ignored the meaning of the rhyme.

When Anne was in her teens, Jim started asking her to dance with him at the Saturday night dances. Even when she wasn't looking at him, she could sense when he was coming toward her, and her heart felt as if it would burst with fear and anticipation.

Jim took to walking Anne home from school. One day, he scratched their initials on a rock. On another occasion, Anne and Jim went berry picking with Jim's family and they became separated from the others. When they found themselves at the foot of a high cliff, they decided to climb up the face of it, until they came to a narrow ledge near the top. They dropped down breathless and lay there for a time. Anne recalled what happened this way: "[He] slips over and lays his arm across my shoulders — my heart beating so — and I can hear his. He bends over to kiss me. I object — then he coaxes, till finally I nod my head; . . . and he does kiss me — but even the

joy of this first kiss is dimmed for me. . . . In all the books I had read, they first told you they loved you, asked you to be their wife, then kissed you. . . . Nothing of love or marrying here."

Anne's mother must have heard about their disappearance because she went out to the road to meet them carrying a buggy whip. She sent Jim away and dragged Anne home. Anne convinced her mother that she need not worry. But it was never the same again between Anne and Jim. He stopped asking her to dance with him, and he snubbed her when they met on the street.

The last time Anne saw Jim Chipman was one morning when she woke up with the feeling that there was an intruder in the room. It was Jim. He had come to tell her goodbye. He took her in his arms, kissed her, and walked out the door.

Years later, she wrote, "But there is never a day I do not think of him, never a day . . . that I have not dressed for him, thinking and hoping he might come."

Adapted from Anne Ellis, The Life of an Ordinary Woman.

FIGURE 6.6 *Parties, like this maple sugar party in Vermont, were another place that boys and girls could meet. While several of the girls are pictured feeding boys maple syrup, notice that not everyone is paired off. One gentleman to the right seems to have captured the attention of three girls.*

(Joseph Becker, *A Maple Sugar Party in a Vermont Farmhouse, Frank Leslie's Illustrated Newspaper*, April 25, 1874, p. 104. Library of Congress)

to keep her boyfriend under control. If you can believe what boys say about girls to the other boys, some girls were not very successful in keeping boys from sexually harassing them. In 1834, New Englander Charles Everett wrote to his friend Elias Nason, boasting that he had gotten away with "putting his hands where they should not be" twice. The second time, he was in church — "Sitting beside a young lady . . . I passed my hand through armholes of her and my cloak and had a very interesting meeting, but she, owing to my feeling so affectionately, told me to take it out but I . . . felt on til meeting was done."

While boys were more likely to get away with flirting or having several girlfriends, girls who did the same things risked acquiring a bad reputation. This double standard still exists today, but the consequences of having a bad reputation were much more serious 150 years ago. It could cause a girl to lose her job, her friends, and even the support and protection of her family. It could also mean that respectable boys would have nothing to do with her.

Young people were expected to exercise a great deal of self-control when it came to relations with the opposite sex. Fear of pregnancy, scandal, and ruin kept their passions in check. Still, innocent games that afforded close contact were very popular. "Bundling" was a New England custom in which a young man and young woman who were courting spent the night in the same bed, fully dressed and with a board between them, in order to have a chance to become better acquainted. Though this practice was out of fashion by the time of the American Revolution, kissing games like "post office" were popular.

DID SLAVES EVER HAVE FUN?

Even when they were playing, African-American children were not allowed to forget that they were slaves and their lives were not their own. Their play, like almost everything else in their lives, depended on their masters. One former slave interviewed during the Great Depression said that on the plantation where she grew up, the master did not want his slaves to have any time to themselves. To make up for the lack of free time, parents let their children run and play once it was dark and the master was in bed. Since they had no clocks, parents watched the night sky and called their children to come to bed when certain stars set.

Several former slaves told interviewers that they were ordered to play by their masters, who thought it was fun to watch them. George Womble of Georgia recalled, "There were some days when the master called them all to his back yard and told them they could have a frolic. While they danced and sang the master and his family sat and looked on." Some masters liked to bet on their slaves' games — footraces, wrestling matches, and even marbles.

Most children managed to sneak some fun into their lives, even under the brutal conditions of slavery. Boys pitched horseshoes, jumped over poles, played marbles, and ran races. They made stilts and walked on them, and they dared each other to jump over creeks or from one branch of a tree to another. Girls made dolls out of scraps of fabric and played house or church with them. They skipped rope, played hopscotch, and made up songs.

It was not at all unusual for the master's children to play with the slave children. One former slave recalled that her master's children played with her and the other slave children all the time, but the white children were always the bosses. Sometimes the white children ordered slave children to do things they were afraid to do or were forbidden to do themselves. Thomas Cole, who was a slave in Jackson County, Alabama, was badly hurt when he jumped off the barn because his master's sons told him to.

On plantations where there were lots of children, slave children would play the same chase and tag and singing games as those played by other American children. Sometimes they would add their own twist to these games. On one plantation, for example, the children would draw a big circle on the ground and form a ring while clapping their hands in rhythm and chanting, "My old mistress promised me, before she dies she would set me free. Now she's dead and gone to hell, I hope the devil will burn her well."

Many former slaves remembered playing chase and tag games like "hide the switch," in which a thin, flexible stick used for hitting was hidden and the boy or girl who found it ran after the others and tried to hit them with it. Another favorite was "ante over," a game in which there were two teams, one on each side of a low building. The children on one side of the building tossed a ball over the roof to the children on the other side. If someone caught the ball, everyone on their team ran around the building and tried to tag the players on the other team. Tagged players became members of the team that had tagged them.

SATURDAY NIGHT PARTIES IN THE SLAVE QUARTERS

Everyone, but especially the teenagers, looked forward to Saturday night parties. To get themselves ready for these parties, girls prettied themselves up using dried chinaberries for rouge, putting ribbons in their hair, and hiding sweet-smelling flowers in their bodices.

The parties were held in a slave cabin, the yard, or even the woods and were organized by the slaves themselves. Telling stories that were scary enough to make a person's hair stand on end was part of the fun. Everyone listened with smiles and understanding nods to trickster tales in which a weak creature like a rabbit would outsmart a powerful creature like a wolf.

Musicians would bring fiddles and guitars and everyone

FIGURE 6.7 *Saturday night parties which included dancing, bragging contests, and storytelling were a break from the grinding labor that was imposed on slaves during the week. This engraving shows friends standing around and watching as two slaves dance to the accompaniment of a banjo.*

(*American Home Scenes, Harper's Weekly,* 1861. New York Historical Society, Peters Collection)

would dance. When there were no musical instruments, the partygoers would make their own music by clapping their hands, tapping their feet, or banging on tin buckets.

Betty Jones, a former slave, recalled the dancing at the Saturday night parties in the slave quarters: "Every gal with her beau and such music! Had two fiddles, two tangerines, two banjos, and two sets of bones. Was a boy named Joe who used to whistle, too. Them devilish boys would get out in the middle of the flo' and me. . . . Set a glass of water on my head and the boys would bet on it. I had a great wreath roun' my head an' a big ribbon bow each side, and didn't waste a drop of water on one of 'em."

As the evening wore on and parents and younger children drifted off to bed, the teenagers and young adults played kissing games like "In the Well." A boy would call out, "I'm in the well!" and the girls would ask, "How many feet deep?" The boy answered, telling them the depth. Then the girls asked, "Who will you have to pull you out?" The boy named a girl, and the girl who was named to rescue him gave him the number of kisses that equaled the depth he had called.

COURTING AND MARRYING IN THE SLAVE QUARTERS

Many young men and young women got together at these Saturday evening parties in the slave quarters and began their courtship there. A young man who was courting a girl would bring her small gifts like a packet of needles, a spool of thread, or a fish that he had caught. He would try to sweet-talk the girl by paying her extravagant compliments. He would also try to make her laugh by showing off his wit and talent for making up rhymes and songs. He might even use charms and "magical" potions to make the girl he loved love him.

Some young men had to ask the young woman's parents for permission to marry her, in addition to asking her owner. Some slave owners arranged the marriages of their slaves. Rose Williams recalled that when she told her master that she would not live with the man he had chosen for her, he said, "Woman, I's pay big money for you, and I's done that for the cause I wants you to raise me children. I's put you to live with Rufus for that purpose. Now, if you doesn't want whipping at the stake, you do what I wants." Rose thought it over. She did not want to be whipped. Besides, her master had bought her off the block and saved her from being separated from her parents and she felt she owed him something for that, so she agreed.

White ministers officiated at the weddings of some slaves, although many slaves preferred to be married by their own preachers. But when slave owners performed a marriage ceremony for their slaves, they left out the words "till death do you part," which did not go unnoticed by the slave community. The slave owners knew they might separate the couple by selling the husband or wife. A former slave named Matthew Jarred commented, "Don't mean nothing 'less you say, 'What God has jined, cain no man pull asunder.' But day never would say dat. Just say, 'Now you married.'"

SERIOUS PLAY

Native Americans were serious about play in a way that white people and African Americans were not. Games and sports were more than just a break from life for them. They were a way to prepare for life. Athletic contests and feats of endurance and strength were also part of the rituals and ceremonies surrounding birth, death, and healing. Athletes trained hard for these events and prepared themselves spiritually to compete by avoiding certain foods that they thought would make them weak and by eating foods they believed would make them strong. All-night vigils before games were not unusual.

FIGURE 6.8 *This illustration shows an African-American soldier at Vicksburg, Mississippi being married by Chaplain Warren of the Freedman's Bureau. Since slaves could not enter into legal contracts, their marriages were not considered legal. After the Civil War, many ex-slaves remarried to make their unions legal.*

(Marriage of an African-American Soldier at Vicksburg, Harper's Weekly, June 30, 1866, p.412. Photographs and Prints Division, Schomburg Center for Research in Black Culture, The New York Public Library, Astor, Lenox and Tilden Foundations)

Parents in many different tribes believed that play is training for life. We are told, for example, that Ojibway parents encouraged their sons to play hide-and-seek because they believed the game gave them practice in diverting, searching for and evading others and that these skills were useful in war. Ojibway boys also played a game called "hunting buffalo," which gave them practice in the maneuvers that they would need in raiding enemy camps. In this game, a few good runners would be sent out on the open prairie with a supply of meat and another group of boys would try to capture the meat from them.

Since Native Americans are not a single group of people (there are more than three hundred different Native American languages), it is not surprising that different tribes played different games. The game of lacrosse, which European Americans adopted from Native Americans, was popular among the Sioux, for example, as was shinny (ice hockey). Neither of these games was played in the Southwest.

Marksmanship was prized by all tribes, but the ability to hit a moving target was especially valued. Charles Eastman, a Dakota Sioux, remembered that when he was a boy, they practiced this skill by having arrow-shooting contests. Boys would divide into squads and choose sides. Then one person would shoot an arrow into the air and, before it fell to the ground, the other boys would shoot at it.

Men and boys who could run long distances were also widely admired. In the Southwest, boys trained from an early age to become runners. In one running game, two teams stood facing each other with the finish line an equal distance between them. At a signal, each team would run toward the other to see who would cross the line first. The game was also a test of courage

WAHEENEE, a Hidatsa Girl, MARRIES

*W*aheenee was a member of the Hidatsa tribe that lived in North Dakota in the middle of the nineteenth century. When she was eighteen years old, a man named Hanging Stone came into her family's lodge to ask her father's permission for his stepson Magpie to marry Waheenee.

That afternoon, Hanging Stone and his relatives brought four horses, with good bridles and flintlock guns, to Waheenee's family's lodge. On the back of each horse was a blanket and several yards of expensive calico. Waheenee's father refused the gifts, saying, "My daughter is too young to marry. When she is older I may be willing."

Hanging Stone returned a few days later and, as before, he brought with him three guns, cloth, and four horses. But this time two of the horses were hunting horses — horses that were fast enough to overtake a buffalo. A family that had a hunting horse always had plenty of meat. Seeing that Magpie had his heart set on this marriage, Waheenee's father reconsidered. But first he consulted his wives, who told him to do as he thought best.

He told Waheenee, "My daughter, I have tried to raise you right. I have hunted and worked hard to give you food to eat. Now I want you to take my advice. Take this man for your husband. Try always to love him. . . . Try not to do anything that will make him angry."

Waheenee agreed, and six days later the bride's family carried a feast to Hanging Stone's lodge. After the wedding feast, Waheenee built a couch for herself and her new husband. When it was finished, her mother told her, "Go and call your husband . . . [S]ay, 'I want you to come to my father's lodge.' . . . Go boldly and have no fear."

Waheenee did as she was told, and in this way she was married to Magpie.

Adapted from Gilbert L. Wilson, Waheenee: An Indian Girl's Story Told By Herself.

FIGURE 6.9 *A lacrosse game between two different tribal groups or between two different villages was like a modern-day college football game, except that there were many more participants and many fewer people observing the game.*

(Caitlin, Photo Courtesy of The Edward E. Ayer Collection, The Newberry Library, Chicago)

FIGURE 6.10 *Two days after Christmas 1909, this boy lined up his playthings for a picture. He had trains, wagons, soldiers, tops, a ball, a hammer, and a cap pistol. It is likely that his sister would have not had as much variety in her playthings, nor nearly as many.*

(Underwood and Underwood, Library of Congress)

to see which boys veered to the side to avoid crashing into their opponents before they reached the finish line.

MORE TIME AND MORE WAYS TO PLAY

In the decades following the Civil War, increasing numbers of children were going to school longer and starting to work at later ages than ever before. These children had little to do after school, on Sundays, and during the long summer holidays except to keep themselves amused and out of the way of the grown-ups. They were a ready market for the toy industry that grew quickly to meet the demand for more playthings and leisure-time activities.

By the 1870s, the toy industry had grown beyond making cheap playthings like toy drums, paper dolls, and board games. Roller skates, which were invented in 1878, and bicycles, which became fashionable in the 1880s, were originally made for grown-ups, but they were almost immediately adapted for children's use. By the beginning of the twentieth century, cheap manufactured toys were for sale everywhere.

Toy makers advertised many of their toys as "educational" because they mimicked grown-up activities. Parents bought dolls, as well as cradles, carriages, miniature stoves, dishes, and toy jewelry, to "prepare" their daughters for futures as wives and mothers. They gave their sons toy trains, cars and airplanes, cameras, printing presses, construction sets, chemistry sets, and guns. A wider variety of toys was available for boys because many more occupations were open to men than women at the time.

In the early twentieth century, grown-ups also tried to influence how children spent their free time by building playgrounds that were supervised by adults to keep city children off the street and out of mischief and harm's way. And in

FIGURE 6.11 *This 1907 advertisement is for The Butterick Rag
Doll, "which is designed to teach the future mother to dress the
future child." The ad advises, "Remember it is but a step for the
little ones from the making of pretty clothes for their dollies to
the more useful accomplishment of making dainty garments for
themselves and others."*

(*The Delineator*, Dec. 1907, p. 1085. Library of Congress)

FIGURE 6.12 *One of the most popular amusements for people of all ages was
watching and playing baseball or stickball in the street. By the end of the
nineteenth century, baseball was being played everywhere — from mining
camps and ranches to crowded inner city streets.*

(Lewis Hine, "Baseball, Tenement Alley." George Eastman House)

FIGURE 6.13 *In the early twentieth century, amusement parks like Coney Island were especially popular with teenagers and young adults as places where they could escape from the watchful eyes of their parents into a world of excitement, wild rides, fortune tellers, freak shows, and penny arcades.*

(Milstein Divisions of United States History, Local History & Genealogy, The New York Public Library, Astor, Lenox and Tilden Foundations)

adult-supervised organizations like the Boy Scouts and Camp Fire Girls, boys and girls learned traditional skills while being taught to be patriotic and to respect God and the law. With its emphasis on woodcraft, the development of self-reliance, and survival skills, the Boy Scouts looked to the country's rural past, when self-reliance was essential to survival. Playing woodsmen, pioneers, and Indians during weekend trips to the country was enormously popular with boys throughout most of the twentieth century and remains popular in many parts of the country to this day.

PUBLIC AMUSEMENTS

As boys and girls grew older, they usually lost interest in adult-supervised activities and went out in small groups looking for excitement. At the beginning of the twentieth century, one of the places teenage boys and girls met in New York City was the amusement park at Coney Island, which was the Disney World of its day. Teenagers loved its fast rides, penny arcades, and games. Nearby was the beach, where they could picnic on the sand, splash around in the water, and stroll along the pier. Coney Island became a model for amusement parks in cities around the country. During the 1920s, these parks had an annual attendance in the millions.

SEE YOU AT THE MOVIES

Movies became widely available in the early years of the twentieth century, and they were another place that boys and girls met. Children and teenagers were among the greatest fans of motion pictures. At first, movies were shown at theaters called nickelodeons because they charged a nickel. At these theaters, a boy or girl could watch short silent films with titles like "An Attack on an Agent" or "Adventures of an American Cowboy." By 1910, there were twenty thousand nickelodeons, with a daily audience of a quarter million people, many of whom were children.

FIGURE 6.14 *In 1926, silent films gave way to "talkies" (films with dialogue and sound) and movies became more popular than ever with young audiences. Best loved were Westerns, comedies and serials with plenty of action and adventure.*

(Roy Perry, "Harlem: Children Waiting for Admission to Morning Movie Show." Museum of the City of New York)

Kate Simon credited the movies with being "the brightest, most informative school" in the Bronx in the 1920s. It was at the movies that "we learned how tennis was played and golf, what a swimming pool was and what to wear if you ever drove a car. . . . We learned to look up soulfully and make our lips tremble to warn our mothers of a flood of tears. . . . And we learned about Love. . . ."

Children in the Bronx were not the only ones to learn about love at the movies. In a research study of young people's response to movies, more than a few teens credited the movies for their romantic techniques. One boy confessed that "it was directly through the movies that I learned to kiss a girl on her ears, neck and cheeks, as well as on the mouth." Horrified by such findings, adults in several states tried to pass laws censoring movies. They also tried to put a rating system in place to protect the young.

READING COMICS AND LISTENING TO THE RADIO

In fact, the young were among the most enthusiastic consumers of all the new entertainment media. When the first newspaper comic strip, "Down Hogan's Alley," appeared in 1895, it almost immediately captured children's attention, and soon they were competing with their parents for access to the newspaper. The comic strip started a trend that is still going strong today. In the late 1920s and the 1930s, children followed the ongoing adventures of "Little Orphan Annie," "Prince Valiant," "Dick Tracy," and "Wonder Woman," to name a few. Comic books developed from comic strips. Later, movies and movie serials like the Superman and Batman series, based on comic strip and comic book characters, became popular.

In the 1930s, thousands of children stopped whatever they were doing and ran home to turn on their radios when their favorite radio show came on the air. Listening to the radio was often a family activity. Without leaving their living rooms, children and their parents could enjoy their favorite music, a comedy show, or a professional baseball game. Radios were inexpensive and easy to build, and by 1934, 60 percent of all American homes had one.

Before people had radios in their homes, children and adults were limited to local amusements and shows that traveled from one town to the next. But once radio became widespread, a boy or girl living in Maine could listen to the same ball games, dance to the same music, and laugh at the same comedy shows as a boy or girl living in Idaho. Radios united the country in a way that had never been possible before.

DO KIDS HAVE MORE FUN NOW?

Young people today have more time and more choices of what to do for entertainment than even the richest children who lived a hundred or two hundred years ago. But it is not so easy to say if children have more fun today than they did in the past. It is possible that with harder lives and less time for play, yesterday's children may have thrown themselves into enjoying themselves more intensely than boys and girls do today.

For a boy like William Dean Howells, it was fun to skate on a pond wearing skates that kept coming undone. But it is a good guess that it wasn't the skates that made the skating fun. Rather, it was being with his friends, their banter, the stories and jokes they told, the competition among them to see who could skate fastest, the thrill of flying over the ice and pushing himself to skate faster than he had ever skated, the chill of the wind on his face and the scraping sound of his blades on the ice. And it is these kinds of things — things that you can't buy — that even today make whatever we are doing fun.

In Trouble

A LIFE OF CRIME

Eddie Guerin (1860–1940)

In his day Eddie Guerin was an internationally renowned criminal, famous for his daring bank robberies and safecracking and for his escape from the French penal colony off the coast of Guiana. Eddie began his criminal career on the streets of Chicago when he was only thirteen years old. His father died when he was still a boy. His mother had to provide the bare necessities of life for herself and her children and had little time to worry about Eddie's schooling or his whereabouts.

ddie did not like being poor, so he quit school to earn money. He had no difficulty finding work, but he never stayed in any job for long. The idea of making only a few dollars a week did not appeal to him, and he was always looking for ways to make more money. His job delivering telegrams for Western Union in Chicago took him into private homes and businesses, where he stole small things that he later sold for money. He used the money to hang out in pool halls, where he played pool through the night.

When he was barely fifteen, Eddie was caught stealing a box of silverware. He was arrested and thrown into a cell at the House of Corrections with grown-up bums, thugs, and thieves. The jail stank like a sewer, and there were men of all descriptions lying around the floor smoking, spitting, cursing, and yelling to pass the time. Eddie went numb with horror and began to cry. The old-timers laughed at him and told him, "Cheer up, kiddo. . . . It won't be long before you're used to it. Keep smiling and you'll be all right."

Night fell and Eddie was not released. A guard came and put Eddie in his own cell and left him there. In the morning, a guard shoved some bread and coffee inside the cell. At ten o'clock, Eddie was taken to court, where he heard the evidence against him. He cried himself to sleep night after night while he waited for his trial. He promised himself that he would never do anything wrong again. He had no one to defend him. His family refused to have anything to do with him. On the advice of the men in prison, Eddie pleaded guilty and was sentenced to serve nine months in jail.

Eddie Guerin's lifelong criminal career began as a boy.

(AP/Wide World Photos)

After being treated like a hardened criminal and living among thieves and swindlers, Eddie became a real criminal.

When the trial was over, Eddie was taken back to prison and shoved into a cell that was four feet wide by seven feet long. After lying in the cell for a week without any exercise, he asked to see the warden. "What do you mean sending for me?" the warden asked. Eddie was so scared he could only stutter that he wanted to be given something to do or he would go mad. "Oh, give him something," the warden said to his assistant before moving on.

The prisoners worked at a variety of jobs to help pay the costs of keeping them in prison. Eddie was given the job of packing stockings knit in the prison into boxes. It did not take

Eddie long to come up with a plan to escape from jail in one of the long packing boxes. A man called O'Donnell agreed to help him. At the last minute, though, O'Donnell backed out and the empty box was sent out of the prison, along with several boxes packed with stockings.

When the empty box was discovered, the warden had no trouble guessing that Eddie had planned to escape. He did not waste his time questioning Eddie. Instead, he threatened O'Donnell, who broke down and told him everything.

Eddie was put in solitary confinement and given only bread and water for a week. He was beginning to think that might be as far as his punishment went when one morning two guards yanked him out of his cell. "[They] pulled me along to a place where there was an iron register over the stairs going up to the first terrace of cells. Hanging over it was a pulley with a long rope. Miserably wondering what was going to take place next, I saw the warden come along.

"'Get hold of him,' he ordered the two [guards]. They put a pair of handcuffs on my wrists, put a hook between them, and then pulled me up the stairs and dropped me down again until I fainted. For something like ten minutes they kept on with this torture. Up and down I went, screaming blue murder and calling Mack and the [guards] all the names I could think of. I was on the verge of unconsciousness when they finally hauled me up, took the handcuffs off my wrists, and flung me into a dungeon with a basin of water and a lump of bread to keep me alive. Nobody came near me. My wrists were lacerated, my head almost bursting with pain. But I stuck my tongue between my cheeks, and resolved to show no fear."

Twenty-four hours later, they put Eddie in a punishment cell where he was kept for three months with no exercise of any kind.

Eddie Guerin had been a wayward boy when he was sent to prison, but after being treated like a hardened criminal and living among thieves and swindlers, he became a real criminal. He came out of the Chicago House of Corrections at the end of his sentence angry at the world and bent on getting revenge for what had been done to him. His mother and his relatives had no use for him. No one would give him a job because he had been in jail.

Eddie left Chicago with a friend and started traveling around the country with hobos, thieves, and cardsharps. By the time he was seventeen years old, he was traveling with P. T. Barnum's circus, not as a performer but as one of the crowd of swindlers who followed the circus from town to town to prey on the people who came to see the shows.

In Columbus, Ohio, Eddie broke into the safe of a grain merchant, but he was caught and sent to a penitentiary for two years. The hardened criminals there delighted in teaching him everything they knew about crime, and he was a good student. When Eddie was released, he embarked on a life of crime that landed him in various jails in the United States, England, France, and the notorious prison colony off the coast of French Guiana, from which few men ever emerged alive. His daring escape from the prison colony brought him notoriety but did not end his long criminal career.

Adapted from Eddie Guerin's I Was a Bandit.

In Trouble

Many hardened criminals began their careers very much like Eddie Guerin did — as children. At the beginning of the nineteenth century, city slums were full of boys and girls who were allowed to run wild in the streets and stay up till all hours of the night by their overburdened parents. Though they may have broken the law, the majority of these children were not really criminals. But some were real delinquents. They shoplifted, broke into stores and warehouses, picked pockets, stole gentlemen's watches, and snatched ladies' purses. A few of them were murderers. Most were boys, but some girls were criminals, too.

Like Eddie Guerin, some of these boys and girls acted alone in their crimes. Others engaged in criminal activity as gang members. There were gangs of children that operated as sneak thieves, ruffians, or guides for men in search of prostitutes. Children were also recruited by older criminals to become junior members of their gangs. The older gang members taught the children to steal anything they could get their hands on. They also used the children as decoys and lookouts for their crimes.

CHILDREN AND THE LAW

American law has always made special allowances for children under the age of ten. Even two hundred years ago, children younger than seven years old were not held responsible for any criminal acts they may have committed because people believed that they did not know the difference between right and wrong. Courts treated children aged seven to nine less harshly than they did adults because they presumed that children that young still could not fully understand what they had done wrong. If, however, it could be proven that a child understood the difference between right and wrong, the child could be prosecuted as an adult.

It was not until they reached the age of fourteen that the law held children fully accountable for wrongdoing. Fourteen-year-olds were treated like adult criminals. Like Eddie Guerin, they waited for their hearings and trials in adult jails. If they were convicted, they were sent to adult jails to serve their sentences. There were no reform schools before the late 1820s to which they could be sent, and until 1899, no juvenile courts where they could be tried.

HOUSES OF REFUGE

As the population of cities swelled in the nineteenth century, many middle-class city dwellers became alarmed by the lawlessness, ragged clothes, bad language, and rude behavior of

FIGURE 7.1 *Many children and teenagers living in slum neighborhoods formed neighborhood gangs that fought with other gangs over turf. This gang of boys in Cleveland in 1911 is shown here at the foot of a hill that it had claimed for itself. Like many gangs today, the boys are of all different ages.*

(Bain Collection, Library of Congress)

FIGURE 7.2 *It was the behavior of boys like the ones pictured here that concerned the middle-class reformers who founded houses of refuge and reform schools. In this painting, Mrs. McCormack has grabbed hold of a shoplifting boy in front of her general store, while another boy who has gotten away jeers at her.*

(D.O. Browere, 1844, Fenimore Art Museum, Cooperstown, New York)

slum children. They saw these children as a threat to society and worried that they would grow up to be hardened criminals. In the 1820s, groups of civic-minded men (at that time, few women participated in civic life) came together in New York, Boston, and Philadelphia to consider the problem of children's lawlessness. These men founded the first reform schools, which they called houses of refuge.

The founders of houses of refuge did not see much difference between slum children who ran wild in the streets and children who had actually committed crimes. They looked on all of them as juvenile delinquents.

Although the men who founded the first houses of refuge maintained that these children were a menace, they did not believe that they were born bad and nothing could be done to change them. They thought that the children misbehaved because they came from a bad environment. All they had to do to turn them into hardworking, law-abiding citizens was to remove them from the bad environment in which they lived, give them religious training, and teach them to work.

These reformers also wanted to keep children away from jails. They knew that boys like Josiah Flynt, who stole a horse when he was sixteen years old, were impressed by the stories of the criminals they met in jail and learned from them. Josiah described his experience in a jail cell with all sorts of criminals, drunks, and paupers this way: "From morning till night the 'old hands' in crime were exchanging stories of their exploits, while the younger prisoners sat about them with open mouths and eyes of wonder, greedily taking in every syllable. I listened just as intently as anybody, and was hugely impressed with what I heard and saw." Because of the efforts of the reformers, it became standard policy in most places to keep imprisoned children and teenagers in separate facilities from adults.

The houses of refuge these men founded were considered to be schools,

A School FOR CRIME

One thief who operated in New York City, known as Italian Dave, was reported to have taught the finer points of picking pockets and stealing to somewhere between thirty and forty boys under the age of sixteen. When the boys had completed their "classes" with Italian Dave, they were sent out in the streets to practice, or they were hired out to burglars to act as lookouts.

FIGURE 7.3 *These children were photographed sleeping huddled under the stairs in an alley off Mulberry Street in New York's Lower East Side in 1890. Homeless children could be arrested as vagrants and sent to a house of refuge or a reform school even though all they had done was sleep on the street.*

(Museum of the City of New York, Jacob A. Riis Collection)

FIGURE 7.4 *These two boys were photographed stealing from a pushcart on New York's Lower East Side in the 1890s. It is hard to say whether the boys were stealing for the thrill of it, or because they were hungry.*

(Museum of the City of New York, Jacob A. Riis Collection)

FIGURE 7.5 *This woodcut of girls sweeping their dormitory in the New York House of Refuge on Randall's Island in the 1871 illustrates how cheerless and grim such places were.*

(*Appleton's Journal*, March 18, 1871. Museum of the City of New York)

not prisons, even though the children were treated like prisoners. Many of the children sent to houses of refuge and later to state-sponsored reform schools had not been convicted of any crimes. They were there because they were judged to be "incorrigible" (simply said, they were disobedient). In 1913, for example, more than half of the young people arrested in New York were guilty of nothing more than begging, gambling, jumping on street-cars without paying the fare, or throwing stones. Convicted criminals were sentenced by a court of law to serve a certain amount of time in prison as punishment for their crimes. But in some states, like New York, boys and girls sent to houses of refuge did not know ahead of time how long they would be there. They could be kept in the institution for a few weeks, a few months, or a few years. It depended on what the authorities in charge decided was necessary.

The uncertainty about how long they had to remain in the

house of refuge made some children feel as if it did not matter what they did, according to the testimony of the assistant superintendent of the New York House of Refuge: "[A] boy who made desperate attempts to escape . . . told me that if he knew how long he had to remain, he could reconcile himself to this punishment; but, that he could not endure to have his mind constantly racked by uncertainty and suspense. He would rather by far be in State Prison. . . ."

The houses of refuge were but the first of a growing number of institutions for delinquent children. Founded by philanthropists or local reform societies with municipal help, they were city institutions. Later came state-supported and state-run reform schools that received children from all parts of the state.

LIFE INSIDE

Authorities in most reform schools and houses of refuge tried to control the children by keeping them locked up and punishing them severely for even the smallest infractions. Children were beaten, sent to bed without food, and even placed in solitary confinement. Two girls who talked during a meal at the New York House of Refuge were laid over a barrel with their hands tied on one side and their feet on the other and beaten on their bare flesh with a six-line whip. A boy who

tried to escape from a house of refuge was beaten with a whip on his bare back after he slashed the police officer who captured him. After the beating, he was put in solitary confinement for three days and fed nothing but bread and water. This harsh regime may have changed the behavior of some children for the better, but there were many others who, like Eddie Guerin, became resentful and determined to get even with society.

In many respects, life in the majority of reform schools and houses of refuge was similar to life in an orphanage. Reform-school boys and girls were made to march from one activity to the next on a strict schedule, and they did much of the day-to-day cleaning and washing in the institution. They were also made to work for outside contractors who paid the institution, not the children, for their services. Girls sewed, mended, and did laundry for outside contractors, while boys worked at making brushes, shoes, stockings, cane bottoms for chairs, or boxes.

It was not unusual for the children to grow tired and bored with these monotonous tasks and then to be beaten for not finishing their work. According to the testimony of the commissioner of the New York State Board of Charities, boys in one New York institution were beaten with a strap or a bamboo cane 2,263 times in a single year as a direct result of

RIGHTS IN
Reform Schools

Mary Ann Crouse was placed in the Philadelphia House of Refuge because her mother could not control her. Her father was opposed to her being placed there and asked the court to release her. He argued that Mary Ann's imprisonment without a jury trial was unconstitutional. In a landmark decision in 1838, the Pennsylvania Supreme Court ruled that the Bill of Rights did not apply in Mary Ann's case because the house of refuge was a school, not a prison. Its mission was to reform children, not punish them.

FIGURE 7.6 *Making juvenile delinquents work was a key part of the program of rehabilitation in most houses of refuge and reform schools. The boys working in a cauliflower field were inmates of the State Industrial School in Kearney, Nebraska in 1908.*

(Solomon D. Butcher, Nebraska State Historical Society, Photograph Collections)

FIGURE 7.7 *These three boys were held in police headquarters for shooting and killing a man during a holdup in New York in 1935. The youngest of them is only eleven years old.*

(Art Edgar, Photo © *New York Daily News*)

contractors' complaints that they were not doing their work.

Some people denounced this kind of contract labor as slave labor. These children were being forced to work for little or no pay, the critics argued, and their well-being was being sacrificed to the interest of the contractors. Others complained that it was unfair competition for free working men and women. In response to criticisms like these, several states outlawed contract labor in reformatories after the Civil War, but the practice of contracting for the labor of adult prisoners exists in many places to this day.

The boys and girls sent to reform schools did not take this treatment meekly. They fought back against the authorities and their rules by running away, rioting, setting fires, and even murdering. The boys in the Philadelphia House of Refuge hated the workshops so much that they set fire to them in 1854. In 1859, fifteen-year-old Daniel Credan, a boy who had already assaulted an officer, stuffed the straw from his mattress into the ventilation system at the Massachusetts State Reform School at Westborough and set it afire. He succeeded in burning down two-thirds of the building. Girls rebelled, too. In 1877, the superintendent of the Massachusetts girls' reform school reported that two inmates had burned down one of the school's dormitories.

SENTENCED TO DEATH

Most children who were in trouble with the law were guilty of minor crimes. Some, however, were convicted of more serious crimes like rape, arson, and murder, and those found guilty were usually sentenced to long jail terms. But during the period from 1790 to 1940, more than 160 children and teenagers under the age of eighteen were executed, almost all for murder.

"BAD" Girls

Throughout the nineteenth century, public attention was focused on crimes committed by boys. Girls committed crimes, too, but not at the same rate as boys. Female delinquency did not become a public issue until the beginning of the twentieth century, when large numbers of young girls began working in a wide variety of jobs outside their homes and earning their own money. Their parents, who were no longer able to keep a close watch on them, often worried that they were losing control over them. A number of parents even brought their daughters into juvenile court, accusing them of "immoral conduct" (which usually meant that the girl was sexually active) or being incorrigible (which meant that she stayed out late, went to dances, or associated with girls and boys her parents disapproved of). Although the girls who were charged with immoral conduct or who were judged to be incorrigible had not committed what we ordinarily think of as crimes, they were treated more severely by juvenile courts than were boys. In Chicago, for example, boys were twice as likely as girls to be put on probation by juvenile courts. The usual sentence for a girl convicted of immoral conduct was two to three years in reform school.

The majority of these convicted murderers were sixteen- and seventeen-year-old boys, but there were some notable exceptions. Nine girls were executed during the first 150 years of this nation's history. One boy was executed by the state of Louisiana in 1855 for a murder he committed at the age of ten; another boy was ten years old when he robbed and murdered his victim in Arkansas. He managed to escape from prison and was not recaptured and executed until he was twenty-three years old. A Kentucky girl was executed when she was only twelve years old. The girl was African American, as were three-quarters of the children who were executed. Until the twenty-first century, African-American, Native American, and Mexican-American teenagers were more likely to be sentenced to death than white youths who committed the same crimes.

Then, in 2005, the United States Supreme Court ruled the death penalty unconstitutional for those who commit their crimes before they are eighteen years old. At that time, seventy-two people were waiting to be executed for crimes they had committed when they were sixteen or seventeen. Before the Court made this decision, the United States was the only country in the world in which the death penalty for young offenders was legal.

A COURT OF THEIR OWN

Though juvenile courts got their start in Illinois in 1899, the person who did the most to promote them was a municipal judge in Denver, Colorado, named Benjamin Lindsey. Not long after Lindsey became a municipal judge, a boy was brought before him who had been accused of stealing coal from a railroad yard. The boy was plainly guilty, according to Lindsey, and had just been sentenced to the reformatory when suddenly from the back of the courtroom came what he recalled as "the most soul-piercing scream of agony that I had ever heard." It came from the boy's mother when she learned that her son was to be taken from her.

Judge Lindsey quickly adjourned the court. Upon investigation, he found that the boy lived in a shack with his mother and his father, who was ill. Like many children, he had taken the coal to sell and to use for heating their home. Lindsey decided that the boy was not a criminal. He was just a boy trying to help his family. Looking fur-

FIGURE 7.8 *Judge Benjamin B. Lindsey with a boy in his Denver courtroom.*

(Courtesy, Colorado Historical Society)

ther into the matter, he learned that many of the children brought before him lived in similar circumstances. As a result, Judge Lindsey began hearing juvenile cases separately from adult ones. He recruited probation agents to oversee the children's lives outside of his courtroom.

In 1903, at the urging of Judge Lindsey, the state of Colorado passed a law establishing a juvenile court. In the role of a "good and responsible parent," the Colorado juvenile courts (and those in many other states as well) had the right to regulate many aspects of children's lives. The court could arrange for adoptions or take children away from unsuitable homes and place them in orphanages or foster homes. The law also gave the court the right to prevent children from becoming delinquent. This meant that not only boys and girls who com-

mitted crimes but also those who swore or used bad language, hung around pool halls or dance halls, drank alcoholic beverages, walked around the streets at night, were sexually active, or were otherwise judged likely to get into trouble could be brought before the court.

Judge Lindsey became an evangelist for juvenile courts. By 1915, almost every state in the union had some form of a juvenile court and a probation system for children and teens. Juvenile courts are still the primary place where children under the age of eighteen are brought if they are in trouble with the law. There are exceptions to this rule, however. In some states, if a boy or girl is charged with a felony like murder, armed robbery, or rape, they may be tried as adults and sentenced to serve time in adult jails when they are

FIGURE 7.9 *This boy was photographed in 1892 at the Silver Dollar saloon in Brooklyn at around midnight. Though reformers strongly disapproved and tried to pass laws prohibiting it, selling alcoholic beverages to children was not against the law for most of the nineteenth century.*

(Julius Wilcox, Brooklyn Public Library, Brooklyn Collection)

as young as fourteen or fifteen years old.

There is no question that the juvenile justice system is more humane than putting young lawbreakers on trial and sentencing them to serve time in adult prisons. But neither the juvenile courts nor reform schools have lived up to the best hopes of their founders — which was to rehabilitate young lawbreakers. Unfortunately, punishment often wins out over reform in the treatment of juvenile delinquents, and juvenile courts and the juvenile prison system too often become revolving doors.

At War

THE STORY OF A YOUNG SOLDIER

Joseph Plumb Martin (1760–1850)

On April 21, 1775, fourteen-year-old Joseph Plumb Martin was helping his grandfather plow a field when they heard bells ringing in the nearby village of Milford, Connecticut. Then they heard guns firing one after the other, again and again. Joseph ran the half mile to the village and found that soldiers were being recruited to fight the British in Boston.

Recruits were being offered a dollar to sign up. Joseph thought, "[I]f I were but old enough to put myself forward, I would be the possessor of one dollar." Other boys he knew put their names down and snapped up their dollars. But Joseph hung back. His grandfather had told him that he would never agree to his enlisting unless his parents gave their permission. This was his grandfather's way of ending any discussion of his enlisting, because Joseph's parents were in Massachusetts, too far away to be consulted.

During the winter of 1775–1776, as talk of war between the colonies and England increased, Joseph, who had turned fifteen, "felt more anxious than ever, if possible, to be called a defender of my country." One evening he went off to the village, where soldiers were being recruited. A number of his friends were there, daring each other to sign up, saying things like "If you will enlist, I will." Joseph told himself that he wouldn't be taunted into volunteering, but since joining the army was the reason he had come to town, he sat down at the table. The enlisting orders were immediately put down in front of him. He took up the pen and, without touching the paper, made several motions as if he was going to write his name. A fellow leaning over his shoulder gave his hand a shove and Joseph made a mark on the paper with the pen. "O, he has enlisted," the fellow said.

"I may as well go through with the business now as not," Joseph thought, and he signed his name.

Though his grandparents had been opposed to his joining the militia, they fitted him with a rifle and clothing. They packed some cake and cheese in his knapsack and slipped in his pocket Bible. Wishing him well, they sent him to New York.

Joseph remained in New York for a couple of months, where he marched in parades and did practice drills. All the while, British warships were unloading soldiers across the East River on Long Island. Late in August, Joseph's company was ordered to Long Island to stop the British forces from taking New York City. Marching to his first engagement, Joseph met men who had been wounded in the fighting, "some with broken arms, and some with broken legs, and some with broken

> Joseph ran back to the ditch, and lying there he "began to consider which part of my carcass was to go first."

heads. The sight of these a little daunted me and made me think of home . . ." But there was no turning back.

After a short break, his company pressed forward toward a creek where a large party of Americans and British were fighting. "By the time we arrived, the enemy had driven our men into the creek . . . where such as could swim got across; those that could not swim and could not procure any thing [sic] to buoy them up, sank." All the while, the fleeing Americans were being showered with a hail of bullets. When the tide went out, Joseph and some other soldiers went into the water and dragged out a number of bodies and guns.

Later that summer, Joseph fought in the battle of Kips Bay on the Manhattan side of the East River. He and his company had been lying in a ditch, watching boats filled with British soldiers come out of a creek on the Long Island side of the river. But Joseph grew tired of waiting for the battle to begin. He stepped into an abandoned warehouse and sat down on a stool to read some papers that had been left lying around. Suddenly, "there came such a peal of thunder from the British shipping that I thought my head would go away with the sound." He ran back to the ditch, and lying there he "began to consider which part of my carcass was to go first." His company was soon running for their lives across a broad clearing under a hail of British fire.

When he was out of the reach of the gunfire, Joseph fell in with two men, one of whom had been his neighbor in Connecticut. They did not know where the rest of the soldiers in their regiment were, and it was a dangerous place to be separated. Just as they were finally catching up with some Americans, they were fired on by a group of British soldiers hiding in a cornfield. "All was immediately in confusion again . . . the demons of fear and disorder seemed to take full possession of all and every thing on that day."

Having lost all of their clothing in the defeat at Kips Bay, Joseph's regiment had nothing but their thin summer clothing to wear as the autumn nights began to grow cold and the rains came. Not only were they freezing, but they were also hungry. To keep from starving, they resorted to stealing pigs, chickens, cheese, pies, and anything else edible they could find. Joseph

Contemporary illustrations during the Revolutionary War did not usually reveal that many of the soldiers were teenage boys.

(Library of Congress)

continued to suffer from hunger, cold, and fatigue until Christmas Day, 1776, when his term of service with the Connecticut militia came to an end. He was now sixteen years old and, "had learned something of a soldier's life."

Joseph took two days to walk home to Connecticut. He helped his grandfather farm for a while before enlisting again, this time with the Continental Army of the United States. He fought in several of the major battles of the Revolutionary War, including Yorktown, where the British surrendered. Along with the rest of the soldiers in George Washington's army, he was hungry and poorly clothed against the cold. Many of the men went barefoot "till they might be tracked by their blood upon the rough frozen ground. But hunger, nakedness . . . were not the only difficulties we had at that time to encounter; — we had hard duty to perform and little or no strength to perform it with."

Yet Joseph Martin survived, and he was still a soldier in 1783 when the war came to a close. After the war, he moved to Maine, where he became a farmer and served as a selectman, justice of the peace, and town clerk. He married and was the father of five children. His account of his experiences in the Revolutionary War was published anonymously when he was seventy years old. He died in 1850 at the age of ninety.

Adapted from Joseph Plumb Martin, A Narrative of a Revolutionary Soldier.

At War

There has been no war fought on American soil for more than one hundred years. American children growing up today may hear about the United States's involvement in a war in some faraway country on television or from their parents. Their parents, aunts, uncles, cousins, or neighbors may be called to go "over there" to fight. Someone they know — maybe even their mother or father — may be killed or wounded in the war. But few children in America today have directly experienced the dangers of war — whether being bombed, shot at, or taken captive.

This is not the case for children living in many parts of the world today, nor was it for many American children growing up in the past. For most of early American history, there was fighting going on somewhere in the territory claimed by the United States. This fighting took place where people lived — on land they were trying to settle in the wilderness, in the countryside, in towns, in villages, and even in cities. Most of these wars were fought over territory, but in some cases, like the Revolutionary War and the Civil War, important principles were at stake.

No matter what caused the fighting, children were there. Some, like Joseph Martin, were soldiers. Most children,

though, experienced war as civilians and did what they could to help their side win. Many of them saw their fathers, uncles, and older brothers march off to fight. The lucky ones ran out to meet them when they came home from war. The unlucky ones found themselves fatherless.

Along with their parents, children lived under enemy siege and witnessed the horrors of battle. They experienced the occupation of their homes and countryside by hostile armies. They saw their farms and homes looted and burned. But as tremendously frightening as all of this violence could be, they were often excited and fascinated by war as well.

TAKING SIDES

In the days before television, radio, and the Internet, children learned about the events leading up to a war by hearing their parents and other grown-ups talk about it or by reading newspaper accounts. Stephen Allen, a young boy living in New York City just before the American Revolution, was taken by his uncle to meetings and public events where arguments for the rights of the colonists were presented. They also went to city hall to see the Liberty Pole that had been put up by those on the side of the colonists. (Liberty Poles were rallying points for the colonists who favored independence from Britain.) Stephen's uncle, who was a schoolteacher, also had Stephen read from the

FIGURE 8.1 *War had a profound influence on many young people's lives. This boy, known as Contraband Jackson, was a servant in the Confederate Army and a slave. After he defected from the Confederate Army and joined the other side, he became Drummer Jackson, a free person serving in the Seventy-ninth U.S. Colored troops.*

(Massachusetts Commandery, Military Order of the Loyal Legion and the U.S. Army Military History Institute)

writings of those who believed in independence, and then questioned him to see if he understood their arguments. "In this way, he inspired feelings of reverence for those engaged in the cause of their country," Stephen wrote many years later.

Children didn't always take the same side as their parents in a war. During the Revolutionary War, Benjamin Franklin and his son, William, were on opposite sides of the conflict.

William Franklin was a leader among the colonists who remained loyal to England, while Benjamin Franklin was one of the signers of the Declaration of Independence.

In general, though, children sided with their parents during wartime. Like children today, they were also influenced by books, posters, parades, and other public events. In the North during the Civil War, children's magazines were filled with

TO ALL BRAVE, HEALTHY, ABLE BODIED AND WELL DISPOSED YOUNG MEN,

IN THIS NEIGHBOURHOOD, WHO HAVE ANY INCLINATION TO JOIN THE TROOPS,

NOW RAISING UNDER

GENERAL WASHINGTON,

FOR THE DEFENCE OF THE

LIBERTIES AND INDEPENDENCE

OF THE UNITED STATES,

Against the hostile designs of foreign enemies,

TAKE NOTICE,

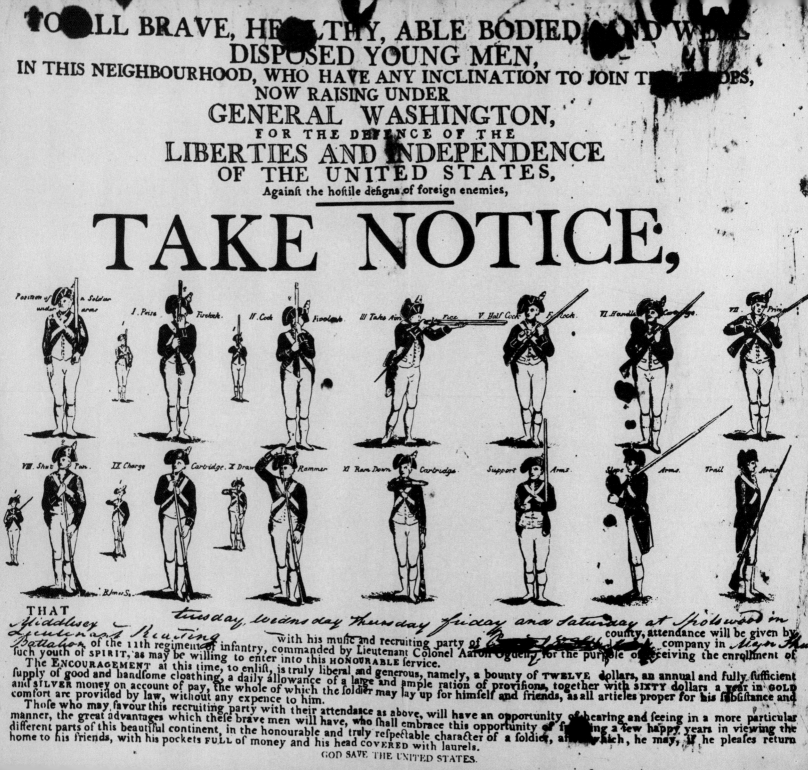

THAT *Middlesex tuesday, wednsday thursday friday and saturday at Spotswood in Lieutenant Reuiting* county, attendance will be given by with his music and recruiting party of company in Major State Battalion of the 11th regiment of infantry, commanded by Lieutenant Colonel Aaron Ogden, for the purpose of receiving the enrollment of such youth of SPIRIT, as may be willing to enter into this HONOURABLE service.

The ENCOURAGEMENT at this time, to enlist, is truly liberal and generous, namely, a bounty of TWELVE dollars, an annual and fully sufficient supply of good and handsome cloathing, a daily allowance of a large and ample ration of provisions, together with SIXTY dollars a year in GOLD and SILVER money on account of pay, the whole of which the soldier may lay up for himself and friends, as all articles proper for his subsistance and comfort are provided by law, without any expence to him.

Those who may favour this recruiting party with their attendance as above, will have an opportunity of hearing and seeing in a more particular manner, the great advantages which these brave men will have, who shall embrace this opportunity of spending a few happy years in viewing the different parts of this beautiful continent, in the honourable and truly respectable character of a soldier, after which, he may, if he pleases return home to his friends, with his pockets FULL of money and his head COVERED with laurels.

GOD SAVE THE UNITED STATES.

descriptions of battles, stories of the brave exploits of Union soldiers, biographies of leading generals, war facts, and stories about how cruel slavery was — all of which were designed to make children loyal to the cause of the Union. Hundreds of books were written for children with titles like *The Little Prisoner*, in which the young hero fighting for the North is portrayed as kind and patriotic, while the Southerners are portrayed as cruel.

Because of a shortage of ink and paper in the South, there were far fewer books written from a Confederate point of view during the conflict than there were in the North. However, new school books like *The Dixie Primer* and *The Confederate Spelling Book* replaced old ones that had been written in the North.

Joining up

All of these influences contributed to the desire of many boys and girls to serve their country in time of war. Historians estimate that there were as many as 420,000 boy soldiers who served in the Union and Confederate armies during the Civil War. During the American Revolution, military recruiters had difficulty finding enough men to fill their quotas, so they did not ask too many questions when boys who were younger than sixteen, like Joseph Martin, wanted to join the Continental Army or the local militias. It is likely that the number of younger soldiers increased as the Revolutionary War dragged on and the Continental Army became desperate for fighting men. In Maryland, for example, one quarter of all the troops was between the ages of fourteen and nineteen in the year before the British surrendered.

There were many reasons for a boy to join the military. Some, like Joseph Martin, signed up because they believed in the cause their side was fighting for. But pressure from friends and families and the desire to be part of a big adventure also played a part in many boys' decisions to enlist. For boys who had to contribute to their families, money was a good reason to sign up. Many boys were aware that if they enlisted, their families would be relieved of the obligation to provide them with clothes and food. Some boys joined the military as substitutes for their fathers or other family members who were drafted but whose labor and wages were needed at home.

FIGURE 8.2 *During the Revolutionary War, a number of boys joined the military in order to get the cash and clothing bonuses that were being offered. Posters like this one for George Washington's Continental Army promised them a "generous bounty" of twelve dollars, "good and handsome clothing," a daily ration of ample provisions, together with sixty dollars a year in gold and silver money and the "opportunity of spending a few happy years in viewing the different part of this beautiful continent."*

("Take Notice . . . ," American Memory, Library of Congress)

AN Unusual **MASCOT**

During the Civil War, the 33rd United States Colored Troops had a pet pig called Piggie. The drummer boys who cared for Piggie taught him many tricks. Every day at practice and at dress parade, he would march out with the drummer boys, keeping perfect time with their music. Sometimes the drummer boys broke up evening prayers by riding Piggie into the middle of the meeting. Some of the men complained to their colonel, but he was very lenient toward them, knowing that the boys were only having a little fun.

FIGURE 8.3 *In the eighteenth and nineteenth centuries, soldiers sometimes brought their families with them when they joined the army. Their wives worked as cooks and laundresses in camp and their children did such chores as hauling water, collecting wood for cooking fires and serving as drummer boys. This photograph was taken during the Civil War in Hunter's Chapel, Virginia.*
(Chicago Historical Society)

HOW THEY SERVED

Many younger boys in the army and navy served with their fathers, sometimes as their servants. Their duties also included being messengers and drummers for their fathers' regiments. Israel Trask was ten years old when he enlisted with his father, who was a lieutenant in George Washington's Continental Army during the American Revolution. He worked as a cook and a messenger for his father's Massachusetts regiment, but his father collected his pay.

Both boys and girls were used as spies and scouts in wartime. David Dodd, an Arkansas farm boy, was the only person younger than eighteen years old who was ever executed for spying by the United States government. During the Civil War, David's family, who were Southerners, fled from their farm in Arkansas when Little Rock was captured by Union forces. A few days later, David headed back to the farm to tend the cattle they had left behind. On the way, he had an interview with the Confederate general

IS THIS NOT A *Tale* OF SCANDAL?

Children who fought as soldiers were boys, with few exceptions. One of these exceptions is described by Rachel Mordecai in a letter she wrote on January 12, 1815, during the War of 1812. "In Petersburg it was discovered that the pretty sailor boy was a lovely young girl, who then made her escape nobody knows where, & it was anxiously inquired about by Lieut Down, who came on soon after & who was greatly disappointed at the loss of his young recruit. This misguided female is said to belong to a respectable family in Baltimore. Is this or is it not a tale of scandal? . . ."

whose lines he had to cross. The general asked David to go to Little Rock and bring back information on the strength of the Union forces there.

In Little Rock, David met with Confederate spies who gave him the information he needed, which he hid in his shoe. On the way back to Texas, he was stopped by a squad of Northern cavalry who searched him and found the information. David was tried and convicted of spying for the South, but the general in charge of the proceedings made David an offer: if David would tell him who had given him the papers, he would let him go free. When David refused, he was sentenced to hang. He weighed so little that when the drop fell, his neck did not break, and his writhing body was left dangling in the air. The soldiers had to pull on the rope to kill him.

CAPTURED BY THE ENEMY

Like other soldiers, teenagers and child soldiers risked being captured by the enemy and either killed or held as prisoners of war. Sixteen-year-old Michael Dougherty was captured by Confederate troops near Culpepper, Virginia, on October 12, 1863, along with 126 men of his Pennsylvania regiment. They were held at a notorious prison at Andersonville, where more than thirteen thousand Union soldiers died from disease, exposure, and starvation. At the end of the war, Michael was the only one still alive of all those who had been captured with him.

Conditions in most prison camps were so bad that soldiers were driven to extreme measures to escape. Fifteen-year-old Billy Bates was a Union soldier who was captured by the Confederate Army and sent to Andersonville. After knocking down a woman for spitting in his face when he rescued her

FIGURE 8.4 *In the days before radios or pubic address speakers, drummer boys communicated the voice of the commanding officer to his troops. During battle, drummers used different drumbeats to communicate the strategy or maneuver that the commanding officer wanted the men to take. The drummer also gave the calls for mealtime, drills, assembly and bedtime, and sounded the alarm when his regiment was in danger.*

(© Corbis)

FIGURE 8.5 *A Southern refugee family taking to the road to flee from the invading Union troops during the Civil War. Thousands of Southerners were made homeless by the fighting.*

(Library of Congress)

from a mob of prisoners, he was strung up by his thumbs in front of the entire camp. "My tongue swelled, my head throbbed almost to bursting and my heart could scarcely do its work," he wrote. When one of the prisoners took pity on Billy and gave him some water, the man was shot dead by Captain Wirz, the camp's commander. Billy was shot twice in the leg. He was saved by a mob that drove Wirz back, and he was nursed back to health by his friend, seventeen-year-old Dick King, who shared his rations with him.

After Billy recovered, the boys decided to escape. They spent eight months tunneling fifty-nine feet under the prison walls. The only tools they had were a pocket knife that Billy had managed to hide in the hem of his trousers, a large piece of sheet metal they had found, and a piece of hoop wire. They escaped from Andersonville on March 2, 1864, and reached Union lines three weeks later. When they were brought to the White House to meet President Lincoln, Billy weighed only sixty pounds and Dick sixty-four pounds.

Not all prisoners of war were soldiers. Some were civilians

like thirteen-year-old Olive Oatman and her seven-year-old sister Mary Ann, who became victims of the ongoing war between Native Americans and European settlers. While some Native American groups offered little resistance to European Americans who were settling in their territories, other tribal peoples, like the Apache, fought back. They attacked settlers' wagon trains, settlements, and homes. Both white and Native American children were captured or killed in these conflicts.

LIVING IN A WAR ZONE

The largest number of children who had direct experience of war were those who lived in territory that was being fought over or that had been occupied by the enemy. Sue Chancellor wrote a description of what it was like to live behind enemy lines during a Civil War battle. She was fourteen years old in April 1863 when her family's plantation in Chancellorsville, Virginia, was captured by the Union Army and turned into General Hooker's headquarters. Sue, her mother, her sisters, and a young brother were ordered to move into the back room of the house. They were joined there by neighbors who were fleeing for safety. There were sixteen women and children crowded together in one room.

On May 2, a surprise attack by the Confederate Army caught the Union soldiers off guard. The firing grew nearer, and the women and children were moved to the basement for shelter. Sue recalled, "The house was full of the wounded. . . . They had taken our sitting room as an operating room, and our piano served as an amputating table. . . . Upstairs they were bringing in the wounded, and we could hear their screams of pain."

During the fighting, the house caught on fire. The frightened women and children were led out of the cellar and through

FIGURE 8.6 *Children among the ruins of Charleston, South Carolina during the Civil War.*

(Library of Congress)

Entering HELL ON EARTH: ANDERSONVILLE PRISON

Michael Dougherty was captured by Confederate troops and brought to Andersonville prison on February 15, 1864. He described in his journal entering the place where so many Union soldiers perished: "We were ordered forward towards the big stockade, moving quietly and painfully along, our spirits almost crushed within us, urged on by the double file of guards on either side of our column of ragged, lousy skeletons, who scarce had strength to run away if given an opportunity. We neared the wall of great square logs, and massive wooden gates, that were to shut out hope and life from nearly all of us forever. The cheerless sight near the gate, of a pile of ghastly dead, the eyes of which shone with stony glitter, the faces black with smoky grime and pinched with pain and hunger, the long matted hair and almost fleshless frames swarming with vermin — gave us some idea that a like fate awaited us inside.

"The guards, knowing our desperation, used every precaution to prevent a break; the artillery men stood with lanyard in hand at their canister, shotted guns being trained to sweep the gates. All being ready, the huge bolts were drawn and the gates swung open on their massive iron hinges, and we marched into that hell on earth...."

From Michael Dougherty, *The Diary of a Civil War Hero.*

the burning house. As they came out of the cellar, they saw amputated limbs spilling from an open window and a row of dead bodies covered with canvas in the yard. "The air was filled with shot and shell; horses were rearing, and screaming; the men were amass with confusion, moaning, cursing, and praying." Making their way around the bleeding bodies of the dead and wounded, the women and children joined the retreating Union Army. They were kept under guard behind the Union lines for ten days.

Life did not get much better for children once the battles were over and the enemy took over the places where their families lived. Marauding soldiers pillaging, looting, and foraging for food left families with their homes in ruin and with nothing to eat. Hammett Dell, who was a sixteen-year-old slave at the time of the Civil War battle in Murfreesboro, Tennessee, told an interviewer collecting the stories of former slaves, "When they started off fighting at Murfreesboro, it was a continual roar.... The house shaking all the time.... It sounded like the Judgement.... Both sides foraging, bad as the other, hungry, gittin everything you put 'way to live on." There wasn't a chicken or an ear of corn left for the people to eat. The Union soldiers took all the horses, except for one. And when they were leaving, they set the house on fire.

After the danger was over, families living in war zones had to pick up the pieces and try to go on living. When Atlanta was burned to the ground by Union troops in 1864, many children, like ten-year-old Carrie Berry, scavenged for food. She wrote in her diary, "We children have been plundering about today to see what we could find." She went to city hall to collect hickory nuts that were being distributed. She also sifted through the rubble of her neighborhood in a search for iron nails that could be used to barter for food.

FIGURE 8.7 *During the Civil War, thousands of former slaves joined the Union Army as soldiers and as camp followers who cooked, did laundry, dug trenches, carried water, and tended the wounded. This engraving from the May 19, 1866 issue of* Harper's Weekly *shows African American volunteers being reunited with their families in Little Rock, Arkansas at the end of the war.*

(Photographs and Prints Division, Schomburg Center for Research in Black Culture, The New York Public Library, Astor, Lenox and Tilden Foundations)

ON THE HOME FRONT

Even when the fighting was far from home, children had plenty to worry about. If their fathers were fighting in the war, the possibility that their fathers would be killed was always in the back of their minds. It was reinforced by their fathers' letters, which described the fighting and the dying. Sergeant Marion Fitzpatrick, who was fighting in the Civil War and who longed to see his young son, wrote to his wife, "But it seems doubtful now about ever seeing him again. . . . Men are killed and wounded around me nearly every day and I know not how soon my time will come." He was killed not long after he wrote those words.

Afraid that they might not see their children again, many fathers used their letters to lecture and admonish them to behave. In one of his letters to his thirteen-year-old daughter Saida, Edgeworth Bird, who fought in the Civil War, advised her "to face the stern realities of life." In another, he wrote "Study, study, study . . . an enlightened, well polished mind, well regulated and stored with useful knowledge, is the greatest blessing. . . ."

With fathers, uncles, and older brothers away fighting, children were often called on to take over some of their duties. George Donaghey, whose father was in a Union prison camp during the Civil War, recalled that although he was only seven or eight years old, he "had to work almost like a man, helping mother to keep life in myself and my younger sisters and brothers."

Blockades — in which the enemy keeps troops or goods from passing through certain ports or territories — meant making do with less, or trying to make or grow what was needed yourself. When the colonies decided not to buy British goods as a protest against British taxation before the Revolutionary War, girls and women in New England increased their own production of cloth. Betsy Foote, a Connecticut farm girl, recorded that she spun ten knots of wool in the evening and felt patriotic in the bargain.

FIGURE 8.8 *Children, like those pictured here, were sometimes so fascinated and excited by war that they forgot the danger. These children have taken up a position as close to the action as possible during the Battle of Bull Run in the Civil War.*

(Library of Congress)

THE THRILL OF WAR

The talk of war, the flags waving, and the sight of soldiers on parade have always aroused people's emotions. Children reacted to the excitement of war by forming mock militia units of their own and playing war. They marched, reenacted battles, and took prisoners. School yards became parade grounds where boys infected with war fever drilled like soldiers and marched to the beat of a drum. Many boys even went as far as to watch battles being fought near their homes. Though they had gone for entertainment, sometimes they came home considerably sobered after seeing the shooting begin and the dead and wounded on the battlefield.

Girls were not immune to the excitement and patriotic feelings that were aroused by war. During the Civil War, both Northern and Southern girls sewed and knit clothing for soldiers and raised money for hospitals by selling handicrafts, toys, snacks, and even kisses at fairs. During World War I, which was fought mainly in Europe, both boys and girls had paper drives and planted gardens to help the country with the war effort.

The upheaval of war also brought the movement of young people from one part of the country to another, and with it came new possibilities for boys and girls to meet each other. Sarah Wister was a teenager in 1777 when her family took refuge with a relative in Gwynedd, Pennsylvania, to escape from the British occupation of Philadelphia. Because sending letters was difficult, she began to keep a journal. Although she mentioned in passing the fighting that was gong on around them, what really seemed to interest Sally was flirting with the officers who were staying at the house with them. On October 26, 1777, she wrote, "the Maj was holding a candle for the Genl who was reading a newspaper. he look'd at us turn'd away his eyes. look'd again, put the candle stick down . . . out of the door he went. well said I to Lydy he will join us when he comes in. presently he return'd and seated himself on the table. 'pray ladies is there any songs in that book,' he asked. . . . we talk'd and laugh'd for an hour he is very clever amiable and polite. he has the softest voice. . . ."

During the War of 1812, seven hundred settlers took shelter from the warring Creek Indians in a stockade on the Tombigbee River, in what is now Alabama. George Gullet and Mary Ervin met and fell in love in the stockade. When George asked Mary's parents for permission to marry her, her parents were uncertain, but George won them over by promising to care for their daughter and to help them if the Creeks attacked. The wedding took place in the stockade with everyone invited. According to Mary's sister Margaret, there were chicken pies, turkeys, potato custard, and huckleberry tarts, "and a jolly wedding it was."

The wars that took place on American soil left an indelible

AN Indian CAPTIVE

Olive and Mary Ann Oatman were captured by Yavapai warriors in February 1851 as their family traveled near the Gila River on their way to California. The warriors killed everyone in the Oatman family except for Mary Ann, Olive, and their brother Lorenzo, who was left for dead. The girls were made to march barefoot across miles of Arizona desert. When they arrived at the Yavapai village, the girls were placed on a pile of brush and surrounded by the Yavapais, who danced around them exultantly, throwing dirt, spitting at them, and hitting them. After this ordeal, the girls became the slaves of the squaws, who put them to work digging roots. Six months later, Olive and Mary Ann were sold to members of the Mojave tribe for two horses, three blankets, and some beads. The following year, Mary Ann Oatman starved to death, along with a number of Mojave children, during a drought, but Olive managed to survive with the help of a Mojave woman.

A member of the Yuma tribe heard about Olive and informed the commander of Fort Yuma that there was a captive white girl being held by the Mojave. He was given blankets and beads and told to go and bargain for the girl's release. Five years after being captured, Olive Oatman was returned to Fort Yuma on February 28, 1856.

A book about Olive and Mary Ann Oatman's capture and life among the Yavapai and Mojave, called *Captivity of the Oatman Girls,* was a bestseller.

The book was especially popular with settlers going west because it confirmed their belief that Native Americans were savages and therefore had no right to inhabit the lands that the settlers wanted for themselves. Most European Americans were convinced that they did nothing as cruel to the Indians as what the Yavapai warriors had done to the Oatman family. They believed Native Americans stood in the way of progress. They did not think it was cruel to remove tribal peoples from their ancestral lands, force them onto reservations, and kill them if they resisted.

FIGURE 8.9 *This picture of Olive Oatman was the frontispiece of the book about her captivity. The five rows of tattoo marks on her chin were put there by the Mohave Indians to identify her as their captive if she tried to escape or was captured by another tribe.*

(Frontispiece *Portrait of Olive Oatman*, R.B. Stratton, *Captivity of the Oatman Girls.* Photo Courtesy of the Edward E. Ayer Collection, The Newberry Library, Chicago)

impression on the children who lived through them. They forced many boys and girls to assume responsibility and grow up quickly. Some children saw so much death, destruction, and violence in wartime that they grew numb. Many of them were haunted by their wartime experiences for the rest of their lives. For others, it became the high point of their lives, a time they returned to again and again in their memories, conversations, and dreams.

FIGURE 8.10 *Playing war is one way children respond to the heightened tension during a war. Pictured here is a patriotic rally on a playground during World War I. Notice the children taking aim at the poster with a picture of the German Kaiser and the girl playing nurse to the "wounded" boy.*

(Chicago Historical Society)

Afterword

The experience of growing up has continued to change along with the country in the second half of the twentieth century. Today, at the beginning of the twenty-first century, American children can expect to live longer than those who grew up in earlier times. They are unlikely to suffer from the childhood diseases that were part of almost every child's experience before the 1920s. They are a more diverse group than ever, and they are also better educated. Their schools are generally no longer racially segregated. More children go to school and stay there longer than ever before. And more children grow up without knowing what it is to be poor, hungry, or homeless.

While these achievements are worth celebrating, they have not reached all children equally. African-American and Native American babies are still more than twice as likely to die as the babies of other Americans. By some estimates, one fifth to one quarter of all American children still experience hunger at some time. Many have no health insurance. Thousands find themselves homeless at some point in their lives. Many more work in backbreaking agricultural labor.

There are several social trends that are continuing to change childhood. Schooling has become more important for life success. In 1940, it was possible to earn a good living with only a high school diploma. Now many well-paying jobs require a college education as a minimum. Children today have less freedom of movement than children growing up in the past.

Rotenberg Family, 1946.
The author is the young girl in the front row center.

They may travel the world on the Internet or travel with their parents on airplanes, but they are rarely permitted to wander by themselves around the cities where they live or ride their bikes into the countryside until they are in their teens.

Families have changed, too. In the past, if children lived in single-parent households, it was likely to be because one of their parents had died. Today they are more likely to live in such households because their parents divorce. They are likely to have fewer brothers and sisters than their great-grandparents did, and they are more likely to have a mother who works outside of the house.

These are just a few of the changes that have taken place in the past sixty years that shape the experience of children growing up today. There are many others. If you want to find out more about them, you might try asking your grandparents about their lives and comparing them to your own.

It may be an odd thought, but what happens to you and your friends now will one day be part of the history of the twenty-first century. You will be one of the children in those "old photographs" that your great-grandchildren will look at and wonder about.

Citations

Chapter 1

Daniel Drake: "We might be destroyed; but another and purer emotion. . . ." is from Drake, p. 124.

"The visit of a boy . . ." is from Drake, p. 176.

"The Bible forbids this, and commands that . . ." is from Drake, p. 111.

"to treat anything"... is from Drake, p. 111.

Anne Ellis: "except that I have seen her love the latest baby . . . " is from Ellis, p. 82.

Cyrus Walker: "I don't want to say please . . ." quoted in Degler, p. 90.

Frederick Douglass: "I never saw my mother, to know her as such . . ." is from Douglass, pp. 13–14.

Caroline Hunter, "During slavery . . ." interviewed by Thelma Dunston, Portsmouth, Virginia January 8, 1937, WPA Slave Narratives, "American Memory," Library of Congress.

"Oh that I could be a girl forever," found in Clement, p. 54.

Samuel Slater's ad for factory hands in the *Massachusetts Spy*, found in Bremner, Volum I, p. 177.

Jacob Stroyer: "for I cannot do anything . . ." quoted in Mintz and Kellogg, p. 71.

Chapter 2

Julia Silverman: "My dearest babies . . ." is from Scully, p. 49.

Sarah Sander: "we put on a grey long-legged union suit . . ." quoted in Polster, pp. 99–100.

Edward Dahlberg: "The fighters . . . would sneak out at night . . ." quoted in Polster, p. 136.

"I refused to go home with two different . . ." quoted in Holt, p. 49.

"I went to school, church, and had . . ." quoted in Holt, p. 120.

"They never touched me or said . . ." quoted in Holt, p. 138.

Charlotte Sander: "My dear Mother, it is not here . . ." quoted in Polster, p. 100.

Robert Chaney: "If I were a strong, healthy boy like you . . ." quoted in Uys, p. 54.

Tiny Boland: "None of us knew anything about riding freight trains . . ." quoted in Uys, p. 139.

Statistics on the likelihood of being orphaned, from Uhlenberg.

Chapter 3

Ida Wells: "Jim and Lizzie Wells have both died . . ." is from Ida Wells, p. 11.

"Somebody has to do it . . ." is from Ida Wells, p. 12.

Child death statistics found in Uhlenberg; R. V. Wells, 1982; C. R. King, 1993.

Augusta Dodge: "Her cry of agony was not human . . ." quoted in West, *Growing Up with the Country*. p. 240.

William Dean Howells: "On Friday, just before school . . ." is from Howells, pp. 195–196.

"It must be distinctly understood . . ." quoted in Tyack and Hansot, p. 194.

John Gunn: "If you would enjoy . . ." is from Gunn, p. 108.

Chapter 4

Rose Gollup: "A tall, dark beadless man . . ." is from Cohen, pp. 108–113.

"Is this what I have come to America for . . ." is from Cohen, p. 159.

Lucy Larcom: "I thought it would be a pleasure . . ." is from Larcom, p. 153.

Hamlin Garland: "I drove my horses into the field . . ." is from Garland, p. 86.

Maria Foster: "Ma put us girls to work early . . ." quoted in Brown, p. 59.

Henry James: "used to pack water to . . ." quoted in Webber, p. 21.

Mary Reynolds: "That old woman would be frantic . . ." quoted in Webber, p. 23.

Harriet Hanson: "I worked first in the spinning-room . . ." is from Robinson, p. 19.

"I don't care what you do . . ." is from Robinson, p. 52.

Waheenee: "My mothers began to teach me household . . ." is from Wilson, p. 90.

Geronimo: "We went to the field with . . ." is from Barrett, p. 59.

Chapter 5

"Sweet are the uses of adversity . . ." quoted in Guerrero, p. 59. (From William Shakespeare, *As You Like It*, Act II, Scene 1.)

Lucy Larcom: anecdotes are from Larcom, p. 151.

Hamlin Garland: "always too hot or too cold . . ." is from Garland, p. 115.

Daniel Drake: anecdote is from Drake, p. 152.

"Rab sees the frog. Can the frog see Rab?" is from Lesson VII, *McGuffey's Eclectic Primer*, p. 18.

"The Village Blacksmith" is from Lesson XLVI, *McGuffey's Fifth Eclectic Reader*, p. 154.

"peculiar physical, mental, and moral structure . . ." Report of the Primary School Committee, quoted in Bremner, vol. 1, p. 528.

Frederick Douglass: "A nigger should know nothing but . . ." is from Douglass, p. 31, 34, 37.

Lone Foot: "It was very cold that day . . ." quoted in Nabokov, p. 221.

Marie Jastrow: "I had no choice but to learn . . ." is from Jastrow, p. 80.

Harry Golden: "When the teacher says, 'Good morning' . . ." is from Golden p. 45.

Kate Simon: anecdote is adapted from Simon, p. 7.

William Dean Howells: anecdote is adapted from Howells, pp. 65–66.

Americanizing name anecdote is adapted from Covello and D'Agistino, pp. 29–31.

"[A] white man — what you call an Indian Agent — came . . ." quoted in Nabokov, pp. 221–222.

Chapter 6

Lucy Larcom: "We were not occupied more than half . . ." is from Larcom, p. 154.

Daniel Drake: "Harvest was a kind of frolic . . ." is from Drake, pp. 55–56.

Anne Ellis: "Any one coming to see me had his courage . . ." is from Ellis, p. 142.

Eliza Southgate Bowne: "The prevailing propensity this winter is match-making . . ." is from Bowne, p. 90.

Charles Everett: "putting his hands where they should not be . . ." quoted in Rothman, p. 52.

George Womble: "There were some days when the master . . ." quoted in Mergen, p. 51.

"My old mistress promised me . . ." quoted in Clement, p. 175.

Betty Jones: "Every gal with her beau . . ." quoted in Genovese, p. 572.

Rose Williams: "Woman, I's pay big money . . ." quoted in Botkin, p. 162.

Matthew Jarred: "Don't mean nothing 'less you say . . ." quoted in Webber, p. 82.

Kate Simon: "the brightest, most informative school . . ." is from Simon, p. 44.

"it was directly through the movies . . ." quoted in Sklar, p. 138.

Anne Ellis: "[He] slips over and lays his arm across my shoulders . . ." is from Ellis, p. 146.

"But there is never a day . . ." is from Ellis, p. 157.

Waheenee: "Go and call your husband . . ." is from Wilson, p. 125.

Chapter 7

Eddie Guerin: "'Get hold of him,' he ordered . . ." is from Guerin, pp. 5–13.

Josiah Flynt: "From morning till night the 'old hands' in crime . . ." is from Flynt, p. 82.

Benjamin Lindsey: "the most soul-piercing scream of agony . . ." quoted in Hawes, p. 224.

Chapter 8

Joseph Martin: "[I]f I were but old enough . . ." is from Martin, p. 8.

"felt more anxious than ever . . ." is from Martin, p. 15.

"as warm a patriot . . ." is from Martin, p. 15.

"O, he has enlisted" is from Martin, p. 17.

"some with broken arms, and some with broken . . ." is from Martin, p. 24.

"By the time we arrived, the enemy . . ." is from Martin, p. 24.

"there come such a peal of thunder" . . ."is from Martin, p. 31.

"began to consider which part of . . ." is from Martin, p. 31.

"All was immediately in confusion again . . ." is from Martin, p. 32.

"had learned something of a soldiers life" is from Martin, p. 50.

"till they might be tracked by their blood upon . . ." is from Martin, p. 88.

Stephen Allen: "In this way, he inspired feelings of reverence . . ." quoted in Thomas.

Billy Bates: "My tongue swelled, my head throbbed . . ." quoted in Bates, p. 40.

Sue Chancellor: "The house was full of the wounded . . ." quoted in Marten, pp. 7–8.

"The air was filled with shot and shell . . ." quoted in Marten, pp. 7–8.

Hammett Dell: "When they started off fighting at Murfreesboro . . ." quoted in Botkin, p. 209.

Carrie Berry: "We children have been plundering about . . ." quoted in Werner, p. 171.

Marion Fitzpatrick: "But it seem doubtful now . . ." quoted in Marten, p. 97.

George Donaghey: "had to work almost like a man . . ." quoted in Marten, p. 101.

Edgeworth Bird: "to face the stern realities of life . . ." quoted in Marten, p. 93.

Sarah Wister: "the Maj was holding a candle . . ." is from Wister, pp. 46–47.

Margaret Ervin Austill: "and a jolly wedding it was . . ." is from Austill, p. 4.

Rachel Mordecai: "In Petersburg it was discovered that the pretty sailor boy was a lovely young girl . . ." found in Mordecai Family Papers, January 12, 1815.

Michael Dougherty: "We were ordered forward towards the big . . ." is from Dougherty, p. 41.

Sources

Abbott, Edith. "A Study of the Early History of Child Labor in America." *American Journal of Sociology* 14 (July 1908–May 1909): 15–37.

Abbott, Grace. *The Child and the State. vol. 1. Legal Status in the Family: Apprenticeship and Child Labor.* Chicago: University of Chicago Press, 1938.

Asbury, Herbert. *The Gangs of New York: An Informal History of the Underworld.* New York: Knopf, 1928.

Austill, Margaret Ervin. "Early Life." Ts., 2214-Z. Southern Historical Collection, University of North Carolina at Chapel Hill.

Barrett, S. M., ed. *Geronimo, His Own Story: The Autobiography of a Great Patriot Warrior.* New York: Meridian, 1996.

Bartolleti, Susan Campbell. *Growing Up in Coal Country.* Boston: Houghton Mifflin, 1996.

Bates, Ralph O. *Billy and Dick: From Andersonville Prison to the White House.* Santa Cruz, Calif.: Sentinel Publishing, 1910.

Botkin, B. A., ed. *Lay My Burden Down: A Folk History of Slavery.* Chicago: University of Chicago Press, 1945.

Bowne, Eliza S. *A Girl's Life Eighty Years Ago: Selections From the Letters of Eliza Southgate Bowne.* New York: Charles Scribner's Sons, 1887.

Bremner, Robert H., ed. *Children and Youth in America: A Documentary History.* Vol. 1. 1600–1865. Cambridge, Mass.: Harvard University Press, 1970.

Bremner, Robert H., ed. *Children and Youth in America: A Documentary History.* Vol. 2. 1866–1932. Cambridge, Mass.: Harvard University Press, 1970, 1971.

Brown, Harriet C. *Grandmother Brown's Hundred Years, 1827–1927.* Boston: Little, Brown, 1929.

Clement, Priscilla F. *Growing Pains: Children in the Industrial Age, 1850–1890.* New York: Twayne, 1997.

Clitherall, Caroline E. "Diaries and Family Reminiscences, 1751–1860." Southern Historical Collection, University of North Carolina at Chapel Hill.

Cohen, Rose. *Out of the Shadow: A Russian Jewish Girlhood on the Lower East Side.* New York: George Doran/Jerome S. Ozer, 1918/1971.

Condran, Gretechen A., Henry Williams, and Rose A. Cheney. "The Decline in Mortality in Philadelphia From 1870 to 1930: The Role of Municipal Services." In *Sickness and Health in America: Readings in the History of Medicine and Public Health*, edited by Judith W. Leavitt and Ronald L. Numbers. Madison: University of Wisconsin Press, 1985.

Cott, Nancy F. *History of Women in the United States.* Vol. 2. Household Constitution and Family Relationships. Munich: K. G. Saur, 1992.

Covello, Leonard, and Guido D'Agostino. *The Heart Is the Teacher.* New York: McGraw-Hill, 1958.

Cox, C. "Boys in the American Revolution." In *Boyhood in America: An Encyclopedia*, edited by Priscilla F. Clement and Jacqueline S. Reiner. Santa Barbara, Calif.: ABC-Clio, 2001.

Cremin, Lawrence A. *American Education: The National Experience, 1783–1876.* New York: Harper and Row, 1980.

Cross, Gary. *Kids' Stuff: Toys and the Changing World of American Childhood.* Cambridge, Mass.: Harvard University Press, 1997.

Death Penalty Information Center, "Juveniles and the Death Penalty." http://www.deathpenalty info.org/article.

Degler, Carl N. *At Odds: Women and the Family in America from the Revolution to the Present.* New York: Oxford University Press, 1980.

DePauw, Linda Grant. *Founding Mothers: Women of America in the Revolutionary Era.* Boston: Houghton Mifflin, 1975.

Devoe, E. "The Refuge System, or Prison Discipline Applied to Juvenile Delinquents." In *Children and Youth in America: A Documentary History.* Vol. 1, edited by Robert H. Bremner. Cambridge, Mass.: Harvard University Press, 1970.

Dewees, William. *Treatise on the Physical and Medical Treatment of Children.* 6th ed. Philadelphia: Carey, Lea, and Blanchard, 1836.

Dodge, A. "Prairie Children." Manuscript in the Kansas State Historical Society, Topeka.

Dougherty, Michael. *The Diary of a Civil War Hero.* New York: Pyramid Books, 1960.

Douglass, Frederick. *The Frederick Douglass Papers. Series 2. Autobiographical Writings. Vol. 1. Narrative*, edited by John W. Blassingame, John R. McKivigan, and Peter P. Hinks. New Haven, Conn.: Yale University Press, 1999.

Drake, Daniel. *Pioneer Life in Kentucky: 1785–1800.* New York: Henry Schuman, 1948.

Eastman, Charles. A. (Ohiyesa). *Indian Boyhood.* Lincoln: University of Nebraska Press, 1902/1991.

Ellis, Anne. *The Life of an Ordinary Woman.* New York: Arno Press, 1929/1974.

Flynt, Josiah. *My Life.* New York: The Outing Publishing Co., 1908.

Garland, Hamlin. *A Son of the Middle Border.* New York: Macmillan, 1914/1971.

Genovese, Eugene D. *Roll, Jordan, Roll: The World the Slaves Made.* New York: Vintage Books, 1974.

Golden, Harry. *The Right Time: The Autobiography of Harry Golden.* New York: G. P. Putnam's Sons, 1969.

Gorn, Elliott J., and Warren Goldstein. *A Brief History of American Sports.* New York: Hill and Wang, 1993.

Graff, Harvey J., ed. *Growing Up in America: Historical Experiences.* Detroit: Wayne State University Press, 1987.

Greeley, Horace. *Recollections of a Busy Life.* New York: J. B. Ford and Co., 1869.

Griswold, Robert L. *Fatherhood in America: A History.* New York: Basic Books, 1993.

Grover, Kathryn, ed. *Hard at Play: Leisure in America, 1840–1940.* Rochester, N.Y.: The Strong Museum, 1992.

Guerin, Eddie. *I Was a Bandit.* New York: Doubleday, 1929.

Guerrero, Salvador. *Memorias: A West Texas Life.* Lubbock: Texas Tech University Press, 1991.

Gulliford, Andrew. *America's Country Schools.* Washington, D.C.: Preservation Press, 1984.

Gunn, John. *Gunn's Domestic Medicine.* Knoxville: University of Tennessee Press, 1830/1986.

Hawes, Joseph M. *Children in Urban Society: Juvenile Delinquency in Nineteenth-Century America.* New York: Oxford University Press, 1971.

Herrmann, Dorothy. *Helen Keller: A Life.* New York: Knopf, 1998.

Hiner, N. Ray, and Joseph M. Howes. *Growing Up in America: Children in Historical Perspective.* Urbana: University of Illinois Press, 1985.

Holt, Marilyn I. *The Orphan Trains: Placing Out in America.* Lincoln: University of Nebraska Press, 1992.

Howard, Dorothy. *Dorothy's World: Childhood in Sabine Bottom, 1902–1910.* Englewood Cliffs, N.J.: Prentice-Hall, 1977.

Howells, William Dean. *A Boy's Town.* New York: Harper and Bros., 1890.

Jastrow, Marie. *A Time to Remember: Growing Up in New York Before the Great War.* New York: W. W. Norton, 1979.

Johnson, Clifton. *Old-Time Schools and School-Books.* Gloucester, Mass.: Peter Smith, 1963.

Kaestle, Carl. F. *Pillars of the Republic: Common Schools and American Society, 1780–1860.* New York: Hill and Wang, 1983.

Katz, Michael B. *In the Shadow of the Poorhouse: A Social History of Welfare in America.* New York: Basic Books, 1996.

King, Charles R. *Children's Health in America: A History.* New York: Twayne, 1993.

King, Wilma. *Stolen Childhood: Slave Youth in Nineteenth-Century America.* Bloomington: Indiana University Press, 1995.

Larcom, Lucy. *A New England Girlhood: Outlined From Memory.* Boston: Northeastern University Press, 1889/1986.

Larkin, Jack. *The Reshaping of Everyday Life: 1790–1840.* New York: Harper and Row, 1988.

Levenstein, Harvey. *Revolution at the Table: The Transformation of the American Diet.* New York: Oxford University Press, 1988.

Long, Jeff. *Duel of Eagles: The Mexican and U.S. Fight for the Alamo.* New York: William Morrow, 1990.

Macleod, David I. *The Age of the Child: Children in America, 1890–1920.* New York: Twayne, 1998.

Marten, James. *The Children's Civil War.* Chapel Hill: University of North Carolina Press, 1998.

Martin, Joseph Plumb. *A Narrative of a Revolutionary Soldier.* New York: Signet, 1830/2001.

Matovina, Timothy M. *The Alamo Remembered: Tejano Accounts and Perspectives.* Austin: University of Texas Press, 1995.

McGuffey's Eclectic Primer, rev. ed. New York: American Book Co., 1909.

McGuffey's Fifth Eclectic Reader, rev. ed. New York: American Book Co., 1920.

Meckel, Richard A. *Save the Babies: American Public Health Reform and the Prevention of Infant Mortality.* Baltimore: Johns Hopkins University Press, 1990.

Mergen, Bernard. *Play and Playthings: A Reference Guide.* (Westport, Conn.: Greenwood Press, 1982.

Minehan, Thomas. *Boy and Girl Tramps of America.* Seattle: University of Washington Press, 1943/1976.

Mintz, Steven, and Susan Kellogg. *Domestic Revolutions: A Social History of American Family Life.* New York: Free Press, 1988.

Modell, John. "Dating Becomes the Way of Youth." In *Growing Up in America: Historical Experiences*, edited by Harvey J. Graff. Detroit: Wayne State University, 1987.

Morgan, Harry. *Historical Perspectives on the Education of Black Children.* Westport, Conn.: Prager, 1995.

Nabokov, Peter, ed. *Native American Testimony: A Chronicle of Indian-White Relations from Prophecy to the Present, 1492–2000.* New York: Viking, 1991.

Nasaw, David. *Children of the City: At Work and at Play.* New York: Doubleday, 1985.

Norton, Mary Beth. *Liberty's Daughters: The Revolutionary Experience of American Women 1750–1800.* Boston: Little, Brown, 1980.

Noverr, Douglas A., and Lawrence E. Ziewacz. *The Games They Played: Sports in American History, 1865–1980.* Chicago: Nelson-Hall, 1984.

Oxendine, Joseph B. *American Indian Sports Heritage.* Champaign, Ill.: Human Kinetics Books, 1988.

Palladino, Grace. *Teenagers: An American History.* New York: Basic Books, 1996.

Polster, Gary E. *Inside Looking Out: The Cleveland Jewish Orphan Asylum, 1868–1924.* Kent, Ohio: Kent State University Press, 1990.

Preston, Samuel H., and Michael R. Haines. *Fatal Years: Child Mortality in Late Nineteenth-Century America.*

Princeton, N.J.: Princeton University Press, 1991.

Reinier, Jacqueline S. *From Virtue to Character: American Childhood, 1775–1850.* New York: Twayne, 1996.

Richards, Penny L. "A Thousand Images, Painfully Pleasing': Complicating Histories of the Mordecai School, Warrenton, North Carolina, 1809–1818." PhD thesis, University of North Carolina, 1996.

Robinson, Harriet H. *Loom and Spindle: Life Among the Early Mill Girls.* Kailua, Hawaii: Press Pacifica, 1976.

Rothman, Ellen K. *Hands and Hearts: A History of Courtship in America.* New York: Basic Books, 1984.

Schlereth, Thomas J. *Victorian America: Transformations in Everyday Life, 1876–1915.* New York: HarperCollins, 1991.

Scully, Julia S. *Outside Passage: A Memoir of an Alaskan Childhood.* New York: Random House, 1998.

Simmons, Leo W., ed. *Sun Chief: The Autobiography of a Hopi Indian.* New Haven, Conn.: Yale University Press, 1942.

Simon, Kate. *A Wider World: Portraits in Adolescence.* New York: Harper and Row, 1986.

Sklar, Robert. *Movie-Made America: A Cultural History of American Movies.* New York: Random House, 1975.

Smith, Peter. *The Indian Doctor's Dispensary, Being Father Smith's Advice Respecting Diseases and Their Cures.* Cincinnati: Browne & Looker [for the author], 1813.

Stansell, Christine. *City of Women: Sex and Class in New York, 1789–1860.* Urbana: University of Illinois Press, 1986.

Stratton, R. B. *Captivity of the Oatman Girls.* Lincoln: University of Nebraska Press, 1859/1983.

Streib, Victor L. *Death Penalty for Juveniles.* Bloomington: Indiana University Press, 1987.

Sun Elk. "He Is Not One of Us." In *Native American Testimony: A Chronicle of the Indian-White Relations from Prophecy to the Present, 1492–2000*, edited by Peter Nabokov. New York: Viking, 1991.

Taylor, Susie King. *Reminiscences of My Life in Camp.* Boston, 1902. Digital Schomburg African American Women Writers of the 19th Century. digilibinypl.org/dynaweb/digs/

Thomas, J., ed. "Memoir of Stephen Allen." Microfiche in the collection of The New-York Historical Society.

Trattner, Walter I. *Crusade for the Children: A History of the National Child Labor Committee and Child Labor Reform in America.* Chicago: Quadrangle Books, 1970.

Tyack, David. *The One Best System: A History of American Urban Education.* Cambridge, Harvard University Press, 1974.

Tyack, David, and Elisabeth Hansot. *Learning Together: A History of Coeducation in American Public Schools.* New Haven, Conn.: Yale University Press, 1990.

Uhlenberg, Peter. "Death and the Family." In *Growing Up in America: Children in Historical Perspective*, edited by N. Ray Hiner and Joseph M. Howes. Urbana: University of Illinois Press, 1985.

U.S. Census Bureau, Population Division, Education and Social Stratification Branch. "Educational Attainment in the United States." Detailed tables, March 2000. http://www.census.gov/population/www/socdemo/education/p20-536.html.

Uys, Errol L. *Riding the Rails: Teenagers on the Move During the Great Depression*. New York: TV Books, 1999.

Watkins, Susan Cotts, John Bongaarts, and Jane Menken. "Demographic Foundations of Family Change." *American Sociological Review*, 52 (1987):346–358.

Webber, Thomas L. *Deep Like the Rivers: Education in the Slave Quarter Community 1831–1865*. New York: W. W. Norton, 1978.

Wells, Ida B. *Crusade for Justice: The Autobiography of Ida B. Wells*. Chicago: University of Chicago Press, 1972.

Wells, Robert V. "Family History and Demographic Transition." In *History of Women in the United States. Vol. 2. Household Constitution and Family Relationships*, edited by Nancy F. Cott. Munich: Saur, 1992.

Wells, Robert V. *Revolutions in Americans' Lives: A Demographic Perspective on the History of Americans, Their Families, and Their Society*. Westport, Conn.: Greenwood Press, 1982.

Werner, Emmy E. Reluctant Witnesses: *Children's Voices from the Civil War*. Boulder, Colo.: Westview Press, 1999.

West, Elliott. *Growing Up in Twentieth-Century America: A History and Reference Guide*. Westport, Conn.: Greenwood Press, 1996.

West, Elliott. *Growing Up with the Country: Childhood on the Far Western Frontier*. Albuquerque: University of New Mexico Press, 1989.

West, Elliott, and Paula Petrik, eds. *Small Worlds: Children and Adolescents in America, 1850–1950*. Lawrence: University of Kansas Press, 1992.

Wilson, Gilbert L. *Waheenee: An Indian Girl's Story Told by Herself*. Lincoln: University of Nebraska Press, 1927/1981.

Wister, Sarah. *The Journal and Occasional Writings of Sarah Wister*. Edited by Kathryn Z. Derounian-Stodola. Rutherford, N.J.: Fairleigh Dickinson University Press, 1987.

Woodson, Carter G. *The Education of the Negro Prior to 1861*. New York: Arno Press, 1968.

Woody, Thomas. *A History of Women's Education in the United States*. Vol. 1. New York: Octagon Books, 1929/1966.

Yetman, Norman R., ed. *Life Under the Peculiar Institution: Selections from the Slave Narrative Collection*. New York: Holt, Rinehart, and Winston, 1970.

Index